MW01006036

# SON OF NOTHINGNESS

## A Novel of Appearances

# SON OF NOTHINGNESS
## A Novel of Appearances

Ona Russell

To Vicki:

Ona Russell

SUNSTONE
PRESS

SANTA FE

© 2020 by Ona Russell
All Rights Reserved
No part of this book may be reproduced in any form or by any electronic or mechanical means
including
information storage and retrieval systems without permission in writing from the publisher,
except by a reviewer who may quote brief passages in a review.

Sunstone books may be purchased for educational, business, or sales promotional use.
For information please write: Special Markets Department, Sunstone Press,
P.O. Box 2321, Santa Fe, New Mexico 87504-2321.
Cover photo by Reneé Weissenburger
Cover design by Lauren Kahn

Printed on acid-free paper
∞

Library of Congress Cataloging-in-Publication Data

Names: Russell, Ona, 1952- author.
Title: Son of nothingness : a novel of appearances / by Ona Russell.
Description: Santa Fe, New Mexico : Sunstone Press, [2019] | Summary: "One
    man's hunt for ex-Nazis leads to a shocking revelation and
    reconciliation with his own troubled past in this 1940s historical novel
    set in Los Angeles and Sacramento"-- Provided by publisher.
Identifiers: LCCN 2019046932 | ISBN 9781632932983 (paperback) | ISBN
    9781611395884 (epub)
Classification: LCC PS3618.U765 S66 2019 | DDC 813/.6--dc23
LC record available at https://lccn.loc.gov/2019046932

**WWW.SUNSTONEPRESS.COM**
SUNSTONE PRESS / POST OFFICE BOX 2321 / SANTA FE, NM 87504-2321 /USA
(505) 988-4418 / ORDERS ONLY (800) 243-5644 / FAX (505) 988-1025

For My Mother

Advanced Praise for *Son of Nothingness*

"Ona Russell's prose in *Son of Nothingness* places the reader in the sounds, texture, and colors of Mexican American noir post war Los Angeles, a time when good relies on evil and the boundaries between Mexican and American are there for crossing.... The novel colors in and breathes life into the era...."
—Adolfo Guzman-Lopez, KPCC, Southern California public radio

Praise for *Rule of Capture*

"A biting commentary on the uneasy truce between Latino Los Angeles and the city's entrenched political, cultural and economic elites.... Alternating between taut, suspenseful storytelling and lush descriptions, Russell eases her readers into a welcome literary escape with well-paced intrigue, surprising subterfuge, and gripping secondary story lines...."
—Los Angeles Review of Books

"Russell intertwines fictional and nonfictional events in an engaging manner, weaving both the peculiar charms of early Hollywood and the real-life Julian Petroleum scandal into her murder mystery.... The author explores the difficult matters of race and religion...effectively show[ing] that identity and oppression are far from simple issues, and that the same persona can be both a victim and a victimizer."
—Kirkus Reviews

Praise for *The Natural Selection*

Finalist, Fiction Category: California Commonwealth Club 2009 Book Awards

"A story about one of the most fascinating trials of history and told with a sympathy and a remarkable eye and ear for the time. The research is superb."
—Anne Perry, international bestselling author of *The Face of a Stranger*

*Beyond myself, somewhere, I wait for my arrival.*
    —Octavio Paz


*My name is Nobody*
    —Homer


*We are now in this war. We are in it, all the way.*
    —Franklin D. Roosevelt

# 1

## WALKING WOUNDED

It was my parrot, Emerson, who alerted me. I had trained him to peck me on the nose if I slept through the alarm. It must have taken several tries because when I finally roused myself, he was shrieking my name and had drawn a little blood. A handful of seed calmed him down. I rubbed his green head until his eyes shut and he lifted one leg, a sign that he was at rest, although sometimes I wondered if he'd simply caught my disorder.

I put him in his cage as gingerly as possible. His feathers closed upon themselves, his velvety chest barely registering breath. He didn't budge, even when my thumb accidentally tipped his stand. Even at the familiar dinging of a bicycle bell, a sound that usually elicited a gleeful chirp. Dead to the world, he was. At that moment, I would have given anything to join him.

I heard the rattling of the fender, the scrape of the kickstand. I waited for David's three quick knocks and then opened the front door.

"Morning, Dave."

"Morning, Mr. Martin. Here's your paper."

I glanced at the front page:

*SAND STRIKE SETS RECORD IN LAYOFFS; B-36 VULNERABLE TO SOVIET ROCKETS; TELEVISION SET TOTAL IN THIS AREA IS 273.*

The words blurred together. Everything except for the date: Wednesday, October 12, 1949.

"I brought Emerson some of those crackers he loves. The peanut butter kind."

"You'll spoil that bird."

"Can I feed one to him?"

"He's a little sick today, Dave. Maybe tomorrow."

David hung his head.

"Tomorrow for sure. I'll put them in the pantry and you can surprise him."

"You okay, Mr. Martin? I mean, you look a little sick, too."

I ruffled the boy's curly brown hair, careful to avoid his pinned-on cap. "You've a good eye for a ten-year old. You're right. I'm not quite myself. But I'll be better tomorrow."

"Hope so."

"You get a new beanie, Dave? Looks fancier than the other one."

"*Yarmulke*, Mr. Martin. Remember?"

"Oh yeah."

"My dad gave it to me. It used to be his."

"That's an honor, huh?"

"Yep."

"Well, you better get going. You know how grumpy people are when their papers are late."

He rolled his eyes. "Yeah."

Sweet kid. Lucky kid, I thought. Siblings, two loving parents. Normal. I closed the door, turning my back on the sun.

But morning was insistent, its deceptive promise streaming in. I yawned and turned on the radio:

*In El Dorado, Kansas, a birth rare in the medical annals. A son was born to a woman and ten days later a twin daughter. Such a delay normally results in the death of the latter baby, but both are doing fine. In other news...*

There were dishes in the sink, so I washed them. The fern looked thirsty, so I watered it. I pulled the shades open, checked the floor molding for ants. All according to habit. Yet I knew, and would have known, even if summer roses were in bloom, even if George Washington claimed otherwise. The dread, the pit in my stomach, and those damn pins and needles in my leg told me all I needed to know. It was my anniversary again. Seven years now. Seven years since 4-F. Since my rejection. Since the army pronounced me unfit for duty. Like clockwork the symptoms returned, even before the date fully registered. A slight unease the week before, a twitch here and there. The incubation period, as I call it. Not that I'm ever free of the problem. I walk with a cane, after all.

I brewed some coffee and fried a couple of eggs. It was nine-thirty. I had an hour before I needed to be in court, a routine appearance but one I couldn't miss. I'd failed to show up at the last hearing because of a mistake in my notes. An honest mistake, and a rare one at that. But the judge, openly hostile to my brand of law, sent a warning that afternoon: "Be here next Monday, or I'll hold you in contempt."

The phone rang. There was an extension in the kitchen but I preferred talking where I could see out into the Spanish courtyard that opened up to Wilshire. The bay window made me feel less trapped. I sat on the couch and covered my shoulders with my grandmother's blanket, the only family heirloom I didn't want to incinerate.

"Andrew Martin, here."

"Andrrreww!"

I sat up. The booming voice was familiar, the inflection distinctive. And I hadn't heard either in a while. "John."

"Too early?"

"Not at all."

"I wanted to catch you before you left for court. Been reading about your case in the papers."

"Ah. We're on hold for a bit. Plaintiff is sick."

"Oh? When do think it'll wrap up?"

"Soon. Why?"

"Just wondering."

John Beaton never just wondered about anything. He had a reason for asking, but enjoyed being cagey. Maybe because he was a millionaire and could afford to be.

"So what's really on your mind, John?" I said. "Another *hermano* you need me to tame?"

The last time I saw John was at a chamber of commerce party honoring him and his business. His company, Boreas, made airplane parts and had infused the city with money and jobs. Ironic, given that he originally hired me to defend him against charges of wage discrimination by one of his Chicano assembly line workers. The man had claimed he was paid less than his white counterparts because of his race, but I proved that it was because of his incompetence. That kind of case was rare anyway, and would have never even gone to trial had not the Lawyer's Guild gotten involved. Rob Tettleman, to be exact, the same bleeding heart I was currently up against.

He laughed. "No. A social call. Dinner next Wednesday. Our place. Eight o'clock."

Dinner? He was definitely hiding something. But then again, I was his favorite Mexican.

"Wednesday? All right. See you then."

I gazed at the bougainvillea that hung heavy over the metal gate. Dinner at the Beatons? That put a different spin on things, whatever John's motivation. Indeed, with that to look forward to, I might survive another anniversary.

~

It was a month after 4-F that it all began. At first, just a little tingling around my right ankle, as if it had gone partially to sleep. It stayed that way for a week. Then the tingling intensified and spread to my foot, and a few days later, to the knee. The doctor couldn't find anything wrong and said something about it being in my head, a phrase not unfamiliar to me. He prescribed aspirin and a hot bath. After a month, my thigh became affected and then the new and terrifying sensation that my entire leg—muscles, tendons, bones—was dissolving.

That's when I bought my first cane, stylish black with a gold-plated tip. I had cultivated, and was known for, meticulous taste. A well-tailored suit, a carnation in my lapel. So I had no trouble explaining the choice. Plus, it hadn't been that long since such items were fashionable, a sign of status rather than disability. I was a throwback, a lover of old elegance, I'd said. My collection of canes grew, replacing my childhood stamp collection, and I started to carry one with me always, even during respites, which seemed to happen for no rhyme or reason. And I almost needed it more when the leg felt as if it suddenly reappeared, when the atoms seemed to realign and multiply. That's when it felt utterly fake, a prosthesis made of flesh. It was attached to me, but erroneously, like a dangling modifier. I could walk again, but my gait felt foreign. At those times, the cane was my rod and my staff.

Of course, objectively the evidence that the leg was mine was overwhelming. A jury would have certainly declared it such. Exact length as the other, same brown shade, same pattern and distribution of hair. The second toe slightly longer than the first, square nails, well-developed calf muscle. And the raised scar on my shin, the one I got as a kid.

But juries have sent innocent men to jail. And no matter what I did, including stabbing it with a pin, the leg felt like an imposter, a replica. I'd pierce the skin, but the sensation was muted, the blood that trickled out paint-like and tasteless.

I returned to the doctor. He said that in doing some research he'd come across a condition that had elements of mine. "Cotard's Syndrome," he said, uttering the word like a benediction. "Named for French psychiatrist Jules Cotard who first noted it as 'The Delirium of Negation,' in 1880. It's a symptom, Andrew. Some conflict in the unconscious. Manifesting itself as absence. Physical absence. You know Descartes, don't you. Body and mind? Quite a romance. Uh huh. Cotard's. It's an odd one, but I think you have something like that."

The upshot: only a shrink could help. But I'd been down that route before, during my troubled youth, and then, once more, after I passed the bar exam, after my pride wore off, when I suddenly felt lost, when there were questions I couldn't formulate let alone answer:

"*Tell me about your father.*"
"*He's dead.*"
"*How old were you when he died?*"
"*Twenty.*"
"*What do you remember of him?*"
"*His eyes. His smell. Everything.*"
"*How about your mother?*"

*"She's dead."*
*"How old were you?"*
*"Five."*
*"What do you remember of her?"*
*"Nothing."*

I didn't go back after that. All that peeling of the onion. All it did was make me cry. I'd overcome, or at least learned to live with, my problems and would do so again. I had a diagnosis. I may not have been able to control the symptoms, but I could control my reaction to them if I knew they weren't *really* real. Plus, it helped to discover that there were others, one who swore her entrails were missing, another her teeth, another his brain. And those were the mild cases. The most severe sufferers believe they didn't exist.

I guess I should have felt lucky, falling under the mild category. I knew I existed, all too well. Yes, doctor. I thought therefore I was. Since as far back as I could remember, my senses had been acute, at times excruciatingly so. Maybe I'd short-circuited, overloaded to the point of negation. Still, I adapted, learned how to subdue, contain, to use the tumult to advantage. And most of the time I could ignore the leg, too. I walked all over it.

## 2

## FRONTAL FIRE

Even today, my anniversary, I'd walked more than I needed to, parking blocks away from court. Before the hearing, I learned that my other case, the one John had been following, would resume tomorrow. I wasn't surprised. The illness story was just that: a story. The plaintiff, a farm worker with an obvious axe to grind, was stalling. He knew he was going to lose.

I nudged my client. "Not guilty," he said.

The recording of the plea took less than five minutes. I was defending a furniture storeowner who refused to sell a hope chest to a recent Mexican immigrant. His right, of course. But this woman wasn't going quietly. She was suing him, again with the aid of the Guild. She claimed her race was behind his decision, stating that she'd overheard him tell a salesperson to "show that wetback the door." My client had been in business since the Depression and had, in fact, earned a reputation for preferential treatment of white customers. Giving Anglos deals, while demanding full price from minorities. But in this instance, he vigorously denied the allegation, stating that the woman had been drunk and disorderly, first knocking over a lamp and then taunting another customer.

*That*, he said, was the reason he'd refused to deal with her. I was skeptical, but he had witnesses, including, by chance, the woman's neighbor. Plus, she couldn't speak English. She'd made the complaint through a translator. How could she know what she claimed to overhear?

"Anything else?" the judge asked, appearing almost disappointed that I wasn't my usual combative self.

"No, your Honor."

I led my client out, passing his barely five-foot accuser on the way. "*¡Qué vergüenza!*" she said. "Shame on you!" She was talking to me, not him, I knew. I shrugged as if I didn't understand and kept walking, certain she'd lose, resisting the urge to look back.

It was still early, and I had no other appointments. In the clear morning, the city was knife-like. No fog or mist to dull the edges. Normally, I would find that exhilarating. But today, it troubled me, as if I'd be cut if I touched anything. Or bitten, since city hall's tower columns seemed to have transformed into perfectly filed teeth. Here too, though, I knew it was me. Tomorrow the sky would soften and the columns would return to their ornamental function.

I had only one obligation for the day, my usual trip to the cemetery. But that wasn't until later, so I walked to Pershing Square, where amidst the transplanted palms stood a few trees that actually turned color this time of year. I sat on my usual bench and stretched my bad leg. A few pigeons searched my hands in vain for the breadcrumbs they expected. I thought of Emerson as they strutted away, hoping he was still asleep.

Across the square, the Alka Seltzer billboard on the side of Bullock's Department Store marred the view. I closed my eyes and leaned back. Trickles of laughter, a whimpering dog, a distant bus. Sounds came and went.

I breathed in the gradually warming air and sat for how long I wasn't sure. All I knew was that the sun was full and high when

I remembered a couple of letters I'd neglected to mail at the office. If I'd had a secretary, I could have called and had her take care of it. But then I'd have to deal with a secretary. I brushed off the red leaves that had drifted onto my lap and eased myself up.

~

My office was in the Garfield building on 8th Street, several blocks away. On a good day, I could almost run. Today, I'd walk, and be glad for the ability. I headed west, munching on a taco from a stand that had been in business for years. As of a few months ago, I'd never tried it, preferring a ham sandwich from the local deli. But one day last summer, the earthy aroma drew me in. The food was even better than it smelled, and oddly satisfying, like scratching an itch I didn't know I had.

I passed the hole-in-the wall record store where I bought my albums. On the corner of 1st and Spring, I glanced at the Times building, where my name was well known, although not as well as at the jail, where I was a kind of celebrity. The lawyer everyone loved to hate. On I went. 2nd, 4th, 6th. The pet store on 7th called out to me, but I didn't answer. I owed Emerson a new toy, but if I went in today, I might do something impulsive, like buy him a companion, which he would no doubt immediately try to murder.

Almost there. I turned on 8th, musing on next week's dinner. I needed a distraction, and this would provide it in more ways than one. I hadn't been to the Beaton's in a while. Officially, that is, and I briefly wondered at the last-minute nature of the invitation. Then again, John could be an impromptu kind of guy, once calling me in the middle of the night just to rant about L.A.'s lack of a major league baseball team. I finished the taco and tossed my napkin into a nearby trashcan, feeling a little less empty. I breathed deeply. The homemade salsa was potent enough to clear my sinuses.

I started to cross the street. My office was to the right, but I had to squint to see. The sun reflected off the building harshly, even blinding me to its intricate art deco embellishments. Still, I could make out the sailor on the sidewalk. Young, Hispanic, with an outstretched thumb. The white uniform underscored his dark complexion, which, from here, looked identical to mine. I turned to check for traffic. When I turned back, a car had pulled over and he was gone. Seconds. But that's all it took. Suddenly there I was, plunged headfirst into the cobweb. I'd been fighting it. Nearly succeeding. But I recognized the pattern well enough. The spidery threads of memory were already multiplying. I had no choice. So close to the office, I had to sit for a minute, there on that stoop. Sit and let them encircle me.

~

*I'm thirty-two, but Santa Claus, in the form of Uncle Sam, is on his way. Tomorrow is my induction, the first step in removing the stain, the beginning of the atonement. It wouldn't be an even swap, of course: repenting my father's sins by serving the country. But a meaningful one, given the man's deep distrust of the American military. Of the American everything.*

*I can't sleep so I open a beer and pace. I can hear my slippers padding on the carpet, the hands ticking on the kitchen clock. I live, or exist, where I grew up, in the family house in Boyle Heights. The paint is faded, the drapes are frayed. The once bountiful garden is a graveyard. It's a house in perpetual mourning, a "FOR SALE" sign on the dying grass.*

*I pick up the photograph of my father on the coffee table. He's posing in front of one of his grocery stores. Not as tall as me, but lean and muscular. His black hair is thick and slicked back. He's wearing dungarees and a plaid shirt, sleeves rolled up. Crates of oranges are* stacked nearby. He looks like a proud entrepreneur, showing off his produce. He's smiling broadly.

*My father. Liar. Saboteur. Prisoner. Martyr.*

The draft process was a lesson in red tape. It took almost two years, even though I'd passed my physical with flying colors. I'd begun to think that even in death my father had exerted his will, that he'd somehow fixed the lottery, for he certainly would have been against me serving. But the notice arrived in July, and the timing proved to be lucky. I passed the bar exam and was clerking for one of L.A.'s most prominent judges. He vowed to help me start a practice upon my return. *If* I return, I said. And meant it. Bodies were piling up. The war was expanding. Rumors of grim atrocities.

*I'm on the brink of something momentous, for the war as well as myself. Tomorrow is a Monday. The beginning of the week and the beginning of a new me.*

*The mood on the streets is charged. Two days ago a Japanese aircraft dropped incendiaries into an Oregon forest. After Pearl Harbor nothing was surprising, but the brazen attempt to start a fire on the mainland ignited the public. Revenge is in the air. Or maybe it's just me. As far as I'm concerned, my induction is a formality. I'm already in uniform, already striking back.*

*Another beer and finally I doze, but I wake with the sun. October 12, 1942. At eight o'clock, I brew some coffee. I shave and dress. Then I go to the law library. For the first time ever, the woman at the reference desk nods to me. She seems to sense something, perhaps that I would help find her son who is missing in action.*

*A rare hamburger and a short court hearing directly precede my appointment at the draft office.*

*I see a portrait of Roosevelt, hear telephones ring, pass by officers of various ranks. I follow the sign down a bright hall to* the waiting area. It's crowded. Some men chat, others keep to themselves. A few give me that look, the one that questions not only my right to be there, but my very humanity. I've seen it before, am immune to their insults. I tower over most of them, in intelligence as well as height. I loosen my tie, as if I'm nervous. But I'm not. Even when the receptionist skips over my name, I have no premonition. I glimpse medical testing through a half-open door. Bare chests, thermometers, white coats. I catch a whiff of rubbing alcohol. I take two breaths to my usual one, but only because I'm eager. Finally, I'm called, guided away from the others, to the right instead of the left. Perhaps a special post, I think. I'm put in a smaller room. Again, I wait. And then, footsteps. The door opens.

"Mr. Martine...I mean, Mr. Martin," the doctor says, slapping down a manila folder with my name on it. He's a kindly sort, round with rosy cheeks. I regard the folder mildly, even though it's thick.

"Mr. Martin," he repeats.

"Doctor," I say, offering my hand.

He shakes it, but there is something ominous in the grip. He lays the folder on the table. "You were misinformed about your status."

"Misinformed?"

"I'm sure you know what's in here."

The cover gives no hint, but he's right. I do. My moods. My overcharged senses. My trips to the hospital. "That was years ago," I say. "I passed my physical. One of your doctors said I was in great shape."

"Yes, I see that, but the army can't take any chances."

He doesn't look like Santa any more.

"Mr. Martin, you've been determined unfit for duty. 4-F," he says, giving me the notice.

I take it, but it burns my hand.

He rests his fat palm on my shoulder: "You know, young man, there's plenty to do on the home front."

Young man? I shrug off his hand, act cool, as if it's the army's loss. But I'm bleeding. Plenty to do on the home front, compounding the injury with his pitying tone.

The white walls are closing in on me, the poster hanging on the back of the door a lie. "I WANT YOU!" Uncle Sam says, his gnarled finger drawing me in. But he doesn't want me. No one does.

# 3

## SNEAK ATTACK

"Afternoon, Mr. Martin."

"Hi, Chuck," I said to the elevator operator. Chuck was ancient, a former actor who played his current part to perfection. A wizened blend of friendliness and efficiency. He could read faces, sense moods, too. He knew when to chat and when to remain silent. I was surprised when he slid the doors shut but waited to turn the lever.

"Mr. Martin, I just wanted to alert you."

I waited, already alert.

"There's this woman...a zealot of some sort. The kind that begs for money, you know. Rings a little bell. Dresses like a soldier. Came here early in the morning asking about you. She's been back a few times already."

"Not there now, is she?"

"No."

I exhaled. "What did you tell her?"

"I said I didn't know where you were."

"Good, good. Listen, Chuck, if she returns, tell her you haven't seen me. That...that you think I've gone out of town, will you?"

Chuck winked. "Sure thing. I'm not religious either. Twelfth floor," he said.

My office was at the end of the hall. The rent was high, but there were two large windows, and if I twisted my head to just the right angle, I could glimpse part of the San Gabriel Mountains out of one of them. I flicked on the light and was comforted by my black leather chair, a Danish masterpiece that contributed to the room's modern grace. Clients don't say so, but they're surprised by my sophisticated taste. I take pleasure in defying their expectations. Clean lines, open space. I like the finer things and have earned enough to buy them. Plus, I need room to breathe.

I stamped the letters that were on my desk and then straightened a few books, on top of which lay a clipboard with notes on tomorrow's case. I ran my hand over my own tight script, as if doing so would yield the verdict. My client was an avocado grower, built his farm from the ground up. Sympathetic, according to the jury's expressions. A hero out of Horatio Alger. I recalled his face, rough and weathered, with thin chapped lips. But it was my father's that flashed before me. Dark and mustached. Smiling, with his damn crate of oranges. I blinked and eyed my booze cabinet. Just one, I thought.

~

I mailed the letters and started for my car at the Broadway lot. A breeze had picked up, causing the leaves of a nearby palm to swish like a feather duster. My leg was intact, but just barely. I stopped in an alleyway, took my stickpin and stabbed my thigh through my pants. I winced, but the pain was eerily soft. I knew my leg was still there, because I could see its outline. But I couldn't believe my eyes. An amputee's phantom pain in reverse.

I limped toward the lot, glancing at the mannequins in the store window. A male and female in matching pinstriped suits held the hand of a young boy, who, in addition to a cowboy costume, wore a grisly smile. Pumpkins and hay bales surrounded the still-life family. The scene triggered another memory, but this time it was miasmic, with no shape or substance. Still, as I continued on, I felt uneasy. Something besides my leg was off.

My car was old, a '39 Imperial. It didn't match the rest of me and certainly didn't fit my position. But I had a fondness for it, mainly because Emerson could occasionally ride along without me worrying that he'd ruin any finery. Moreover, it provided a counterweight to those who might have confused my aesthetic sensibility with dandyism.

The lock had a will of its own. This time it worked, so I got in and started the engine. I checked my rearview mirror. All clear. As I started to back up, though, I spotted a woman in uniform, a sight that always made me cringe. Dark blue, with gold buttons. Skirt below her knees. WAVE, I thought. A goddamn WAVE. But I wasn't that lucky. The bonnet, something out of the Victorian age, gave her away. That wasn't military, it was religious. Salvation Army. The woman was imploring me to stop, and worse, I knew who she was. I slammed on the brakes.

"Mr. Martin. I'm..."

"You were following me."

"Forgive me. I'm..."

"I know who you are. Miss Crane. From Stockton, right? Here about the girl at that, that place. Fairhaven. Didn't your secretary give you my last message?"

"Yes, but..."

"Well, what don't you understand about it? I've told you repeatedly. Not interested."

"If you would just give me a moment of your time, I think you might see it differently," she said, in the tone of a supplicant.

I couldn't tell her age, but she looked about the same as I imagined her when we first talked on the phone. Somewhat young. Thin. Fair. Plain and pointed with a strained expression. She'd been pestering me for a month, threatening to show up if I didn't relent. But why? And why today?

"Please," she said. Her pale cheeks colored. "It won't take long."

I gritted my teeth, so hard that I heard the fibers in my jaw crunch. I had to get her off my back. I could do it right here, get it over with. But I didn't trust my leg, and I wasn't about to invite her into my car. This needed an emphatic environment, a place where I had power, where I couldn't be misconstrued. "Fifteen minutes," I said. "I'll give you fifteen minutes."

She folded her hands as if in prayer. "Thank you."

"My office," I said. "You know where it is."

~

"Miss Crane."

"Penny."

"Penny," I said, leading her into the office. "Please, sit." I opened my desk drawer and pulled out a cinnamon stick, the pacifier I'd traded in for my cigarettes and pipe a few years ago. The idea wasn't original, but I'd improved upon it, smoothing out the sticks' splinters with a pocketknife until they resembled and felt like thin cigars. People often mistook them as such, more than once offering me a light. I've gotten used to them, but initially they were a poor substitute for Dunhill's cherry tobacco. The withdrawal had been brutal.

"I hope you don't mind," she said, removing her bonnet.

I was startled, first at the sensual way she tossed her head, and second that her hair was long and shiny. A lively color, as well, like sunburned wheat. And her scent was unexpected, too, clean but with a trace of a fresh Lucky Strike.

She tossed her head again and exhaled. "I noticed you limping," she said. "Are you all right?"

My limp wasn't what most women first noticed about me. Usually it was my resemblance to Gregory Peck. Hair, eyes, jaw line. Even when they didn't say so, they noticed. Blushing, giggling, batting their lashes. Before I uttered a word, they were smitten. I was darker, of course, with a broader nose and wider lips. But I had Peck's height and could still pass for his brother. And that was the problem. Instead of seeing me, women saw Peck, the screen version of him. They fell in love with an image. With a matinee idol. A liberal. Sometimes I encouraged them, played the part. I'd gotten good at pretending, could put on the charm for a while. But I couldn't sustain it. I was a darker version of the actor in more ways than one.

I nodded, twiddling the stick. "Don't worry about that. The clock is ticking."

"You know what Fairhaven is, of course."

"A holding tank," I said flatly. "For unwed mothers."

She frowned. "Oh dear, well, I guess you could put it that way."

"Go on."

She lowered her eyes, laced and unlaced her fingers, shifted in her seat. "I lied," she said.

"Lied? About what?"

"On the phone, I mean. This isn't about one of the girls."

"Oh? What is it about, then?"

"Now that I'm here...well, it's difficult..." she said, appearing smaller, shriveled.

I sucked on the stick, releasing spice into the air. "What do you want? Money?" I said, feeling somehow relieved, even generous.

"No, it's...well, this will likely come as a shock."

I didn't respond.

"I've come about your mother."

"My *what*?"

"Your mother, Isabella Martínez. It's a long story. I don't think fifteen minutes..."

I stood up, wobbling. "My *mother*? What the hell are you talking about?"

"Your mother.... She lives with us...at Fairhaven."

A siren's howl penetrated the window. Somewhere, a fire or a heart attack or an accident. Someone waiting to be saved. Maybe a sick woman, a dying woman.

*"Come here, Mijo."*

*"What, Pop?"*

*"Come, sit on my lap."*

*"What's wrong?"*

*"You have to be strong."*

*"Why do you look like that, Pop?"*

*"You know I love you."*

*"Why are you holding me so tight?"*

*"Mijo, your mother is gone."*

*"Gone? Where is she?"*

*"She went to heaven."*

"You're out of your mind," I said, wondering who was behind this. Maybe someone at the Guild. Their idea of a joke. "My mother is dead."

"No. She's not. But she will be. Soon, perhaps. She's ill and..."

I didn't know what this broad was up to, and I didn't care. "I want you out of here. Now!"

She didn't budge, started to speak rapid fire, like a machine gun: "Your mother had an affair.... Your father kicked her out.... She was lost, on the streets, forced into prostitution...and..."

"Enough! Get out!" I said, yanking her out of the chair. "Get out of here."

~

I headed back to the booze cabinet. My heart was pounding, the beats reverberating in my ears. I poured another shot and went to the window. The mountains were still there, reassuring in their indifference. I drank them in with the booze. My mother. Alive? I'd longed for her, prayed for her. Absurd. Impossible. At best mistaken identity, at worse, derangement. I had enough to worry about, like keeping myself together until sundown.

My leg had now all but dissolved. I rolled up my pant leg and stabbed my knee with a pen, the soft spot right under the bone. Nothing. The area was permanently bruised from previous stabs, but I did it again. Finally it bled, bright red trickling down the shin. Still nothing. I shook it, tried to stimulate the cells but it only made matters worse. Again, I knew. It wasn't really happening. But Freud could only go so far. I patted the blood and checked my watch. Four o'clock. Thank God. Almost over. The miserable day was almost over.

~

It took nearly forty minutes to drive across town to the National Cemetery on the edge of Westwood, close to UCLA.

I crept along on Wilshire, fighting the traffic as well as my thoughts. I remembered the night my father told me my mother had died, that she'd gone to heaven. It was late, past my bedtime. Sudden illness, he'd said. I was only five, but I knew what that meant. A month before, our dog had been hit by a car. One minute romping in the yard, the next limp in my father's arms. He was a mutt with soft and voluminous fur that I loved to bury myself in. No pillow, no blanket could replace it. It was that fur that I missed more than anything, the rising and falling warmth of it. Its absence taught me what death was.

A stream of cars as far as the eye could see, which was not as far as it used to be, before endless construction cluttered the view. A sliver of low sun was all but gone, but the cemetery gate was still open. I parked, checked in and was told I had an hour until they locked up. I headed for my usual spot, bypassing fighters of the twentieth century, especially those bearing names like García and Hernández. On my first anniversary, when the war was still on, I sought them out. I felt guilty for not serving, for being alive. I thought maybe the reality of their deaths would arouse some unconscious, ethnic pride, not to mention make me grateful I was still here. About nine thousand Latinos were killed in the war, and I could have been one of them. My alias certainly wouldn't have fooled anybody who wasn't colorblind. But when I'd stood before those graves, I instead felt cheated. I should have been buried under that earth, with a word or two marking my sacrifice. It wasn't that I didn't respect the corpses that lay there, I just resented the men they once were.

Still, I was compelled to come. A ritual. Strangely comforting, yet also a kind of penance. An apology. For myself. For my father.

It was to the older section, the one devoted to veterans of the Civil War, where I went this time. On the western edge of the cemetery, with a groomed lawn and eucalyptus trees shading the sacred plots, it stood as a testament to those who prevented the country's collapse. But the Civil War was also distant, so much so that it elicited no guilt in me. Here, I could honor the dead without mourning my own loss. Here, silence muted the screeching of 4-F.

Every year I chose one grave in particular. Three years ago, it was that of a black soldier, a man who gave his life for a country that enslaved him. Odd, I know, that I would venerate a member of one despised group yet ignore my own embattled lot. But I did, and I'm not bothered by that inconsistency. I'm not a bigot. It's not race or religion that offends me, but behavior. That's why I was opposed to the internment camps, for instance. The Japanese living here weren't criminals, didn't do anything to warrant such treatment. Some of those poor souls were even my neighbors. No, it's more of a personal thing for me. The original inhabitants of California, the Mexican-American War and all that. My father drilled it into me. And at one time, I *was* a loyalist, swollen with national pride. I even associated myself with the Stridentistas, an avant-garde group of Mexican revolutionaries. But that was before. Before my father chose a cause over me. Before my roots, exposed to the light, rotted in the sun.

I glanced around at the wood and granite, the religious symbols and statues. My eyes fixed on a marble stone with scrolled lettering:

THOMAS SANFORD. 1830-1864. BELOVED SON OF WILLIAM AND BETSY. HUSBAND TO CAROLYN, FATHER TO BONNIE AND SAMUEL. A HERO TO THE UNION.

That was the extent of the epitaph. I sat on the grass and took out the bottle I'd brought from the office. Several swigs and the soldier's misty features came into view. Tall and fair, with sandy hair and grey eyes. High rank. Major or colonel, with gleaming buttons on his dark-blue uniform. A real title. A real uniform. A strapping figure, as they say. Sound in mind and body. Member of a long-standing Anglo family, tracing his roots, like John Beaton, to the Puritans. Supported and loved, a golden child.

Another swig and I started to feel my leg again, one more and the sharp edges of my other senses began to soften. Rum. That was my drink, and just then it tasted like a hard-won truce.

I rested back on a spindly tree trunk and stayed there until dew coated the ground and the sky smudged black and blue.

# 4

# TRIBUNAL

The brass urn in which I kept my canes was decorative as well as functional. I'd picked it up at an estate sale, drawn to its superb workmanship. A wreath of delicate leaves had been carved onto one side, a lion's head on the other; some kind of duality, I supposed, that seemed fitting. It stood in a nook in my living room, where the sun, filtering through my yet unopened curtains, played upon its golden surface.

Ten canes stood at varying degrees of attention, each bearing memories. I thumbed through the choices. The one shaped like a snake I'd actually used to kill a small rattler that had taken residence in my kitchen. The one with the silver inlay accompanied me to a near miss with a truck—I'd mused that the gleam of the metal had alerted the driver of my presence. The dull brown, the least interesting of the lot, helped me celebrate the day I won big at the track.

The press loved my canes almost as much as I needed them, often interpreting whichever I brought to court as a sign of my level of confidence in a case. So, which did I want analyzed in the *Times* tomorrow? I glanced at Emerson. "All right. Parrot head it is." The opened-beak tip would amuse the jury, who would also be drawn to its bright, primary colors. I could afford to be a little whimsical today. The trial was going my way, and my anniversary had passed. That alone was reason for cheer, especially because this year had been more torturous than usual, given the encounter with the Salvationist. But even on that subject, I'd come to a decision that had lightened my mood, starting with the premise that she might have been telling the truth.

I'd accused her of scheming, of insanity, but that was in the heat of the moment. In the middle of the night, I'd thought back to her face, less plain without the bonnet, pretty even, with sincere, green eyes. It was startling, of course. The possibility. My mother, alive. An earthquake and tornado in one, shaking me, sucking me in if I let it. But why in God's name would I? From what that woman, Penny, had said, my mother had been a cheat, a whore. No better than my father, whose invention of her death, if the story was true, was perhaps the only thing about him I might be able to forgive. And worse, if she was alive, she'd never contacted me. Childhood. Youth. My miserable teens. Even as an adult, when my father no longer held any sway. Not a word. Her own flesh and blood. So why would I see her now? For an apology? I didn't need it. Didn't want it. She was ill, Penny said. Not long for this Earth. Well, I'd been ill too, many a time, desperate for maternal comfort. So no. No deathbed scene for me. We were even.

~

Judge Clemons, a former quarterback with a legendary temper and Coke-bottle glasses, scowled as he trudged up to his chair, personally designed to accommodate his girth. He hated delays, and thirty years on the bench had earned him the right to be annoyed. He was a hardliner, no-nonsense. For Clemons, there was no shade of grey. We understood each other perfectly.

"Swear him in," he said to the bailiff, referring to the plaintiff, Raúl López.

Raúl took the stand, radically altered from his last appearance. Gone was the slouch, the hostile expression. Gone, too, was his flamboyant attire, replaced with a sedate, tailored gabardine. More respectable, less Chicano. Especially striking was the change in his hair. From oiled and slicked back to military style crew cut. I guessed the Guild wasn't opposed to a little assimilation after all.

"You look *considerably* better, Mr. López?" the judge said.

I smirked, trying to catch his magnified eye.

"I am, your Honor."

"Let's get to it then. "Counselor?"

The courtroom was packed, onlookers squeezed into the gleaming, church-like pews. I remembered the ribbon cutting ceremony for the building in 1940, when architects Underwood and Simon were lauded for creating the largest structure in the Western U.S. Since then, it had fallen in rank, but the courthouse was still impressive. Granite, travertine, walnut. Rich but restrained. I responded to the less is more Art Moderne style.

I usually opted for the central entrance on Spring Street, especially when I was in need of the luck that seemed to follow me there. But I didn't feel superstitious today, so I'd come in through Main, where a painting entitled "Law"—a lithe, young woman with an embossed tablet—hung reassuringly in the oval lobby. This lobby was less crowded, quieter than its larger, rectangular counterpart on Spring. So quiet that my cane clicked audibly on its glossy, terrazzo floor.

The case didn't warrant a trial and normally wouldn't have attracted the public. But my client, George Patterson, was a minor celebrity and the Guild was trying to make an example of him. In addition to his avocado farm in Yorba Linda, he was a talented saxophonist that played in jazz bars all over the city. He had a following, and many of his fans—whites, blacks, even a few Chicanos—had come to lend their support. Even some whom under other circumstances would have probably been more sympathetic to Raúl.

On Monday, we'd left off with me questioning Raúl as to why he'd suddenly decided he wasn't getting paid enough, especially when he made twice as much as the migrant pickers on the farm. He'd answered that he was a U.S. citizen, not a migrant and not a picker, which, of course I'd known. (It was a bit of a risky move, comparing him to Mexican laborers. But I knew this jury— comprised mainly of working stiffs—wouldn't see it that way). Raúl said he was entitled to a raise because in the five years he'd been doing odd jobs for George, he'd never received one. I ended by asking, but not really allowing him to answer, what he'd done to earn it.

It was the prosecution's turn. Bob Tettleman was seated in the aisle across from me. Middle-aged, bushy haired, slender. He rose, tucking in his characteristically rumpled shirt. A cultivated look, I thought. All the Guild members had it, as if they'd been up all night. Working overtime for the disenfranchised, the oppressed. Bob was also always smiling, too warmly, as if attached to the sun. Except at me, which I took as a badge of honor.

"Good morning, Mr. López," he said. "Now, let's go back to Mr. Martin's question. What do you feel you have done to earn a raise?"

Raúl lowered his eyes, shook his head slightly. Then he turned to the jury. "I've worked overtime, for nothing. I've never taken a sick day. Always been there when Mr. Patterson needed me."

His voice had softened, had added a hitch, as if he might cry.

"Mr. Martin also asked you why now? Why you hadn't brought the topic up to your boss before."

Raúl licked his lips, swallowed, feigning emotion. "I learned that another employee who had only been with the company for two years got a raise."

"Who was that person?"

"Josh Barker."

"The man who testified last week?"

"Yes."

"Did you ask Mr. Patterson about it?"

"Yes."

"And what did he say?"

"That Josh had more complex duties."

"The same ones to which Mr. Barker testified?"

"Yes."

"Do you recall what they were?"

"Taking orders, checking the shipping boxes, making local deliveries."

"Did you ever do any of those?"

"Yes. I used to."

"Were they too complex for you?"

I half-stood. "Objection."

"You may answer."

"No."

"So what difference, if any, did you see between this other man and yourself?"

Raúl thought for moment. "He was white."

The courtroom stirred. Judge Clemons gave his gavel a perfunctory tap.

Patterson nudged me but I shook my head. I thought about objecting, but it wasn't worth it. This case wasn't going to be decided on the merits, anyway.

"No more questions, your Honor."

"Mr. Martin?" the judge said.

I stood, sifted through a heap of meaningless papers. Then I inched out from behind the table, deliberately. Cane in hand, I limped past the jury, giving them, so to speak, a bird's eye view. I gazed at the room's walnut wainscoting, the inlaid design of waves and stars, and then turned to Raúl. "You look a little uncomfortable in those clothes."

"Objection!"

"Mr. Martin..." the judge said.

"Withdraw the comment, your Honor."

"Mr. López. Have you ever heard of the Scopes monkey trial?"

"The what?" He frowned, eyed Tettleman.

"Objection," Bob said. "Scopes? What is this, your Honor?"

I caught Don Elliot's nod. He was sitting in the front row. Don was a top-notch attorney and board member of the American Bar Association. The ABA. Right-wing, traditional, powerful. In direct contrast to the Guild, which had come into being to counter the Bar's influence. The nod was approving, indicating that he liked my tactic. This was an audition, I thought. I was on trial, too.

"Go on, Mr. Martin," Clemons said. "Make your point. Quickly." He didn't mean it. I knew his impatience was an act.

"The Scopes trial was about the role of science in the classroom. John Scopes was a teacher who taught Darwin's theory, violating Tennessee State Law. The ACLU promoted the case, saw that it was brought to trial. But they didn't care a whit about Scopes himself. They were using him as a pawn."

Raúl looked at me blankly.

"Mr. López," I said, "how did you find your attorney?"

"Objection!"

"Did you contact Mr. Tettleman, or did he contact you?"

"Objection!"

"The Guild learned from the ACLU," I said. "I'm afraid you might be their Scopes."

"Objection, your Honor!"

"Sustained."

"That's all," I said.

The comparison wasn't hyperbole. The Guild needed a new precedent. Anything smelling of class or racial injustice. They wanted another Sleepy Lagoon, the murder case that had brought them fame. Defending all those Chicanos, losing in court, and then, years later, getting their convictions overturned. Noble, one might say. But they were idealists, and, as in Scopes, weren't above risking the person to the principle. Was López such a case? I didn't know, but I'd muddied the waters by suggesting it was. Tomorrow it would go to the jury.

With my anniversary over, my leg was predictably better, and I was feeling so generally optimistic, that I eschewed my usual solitary lunch and went upstairs before going home. Compared to the rest of the building, the cafeteria was a dismal place, plastic and unadorned. Art Moderne gone overboard. But even that didn't bother me today. I opted for the soup and sandwich, and sat at one of the few, unoccupied tables.

"Andy."

I turned to see Don Elliott's ruddy face gazing down on me. He was grinning, a little spittle in the corner of his mouth. "Nice job. Very nice."

"Thanks."

He leaned over and whispered in my ear. "Keep it up."

I ate heartily, even though the food was as bland as the room. Becoming a member of the ABA would be a professional coup. My conservative credentials would be burnished. The first Latino to be admitted. A token perhaps, but who cared? I wanted in. It would be a finger to my father, too, who had viewed the group as a threat to unions, which, of course, it was.

"¿*Terminado, señor?*" said a woman bussing the tables. She wore a hairnet and had the wide, strong features of an indian. She'd asked if I was done with my soup. I unwittingly thought of my mother.

"Am I finished? No, I am not," I said.

She pulled back and toddled away, her black, rubber shoes squeaking on the polished floor.

But I was, in fact, done, so I got up. At a nearby table sat Bob Tettleman and a few others from the Guild. He'd been watching me. I'd ignored him, but when he saw me now he came over.

"It's not gonna work," he said.

"We'll see."

"Scopes? Come on. Where's our Clarence Darrow?"

"You'd have asked him if he were alive."

"Jesus. What's with you, Martin?"

"What do you mean?"

"The hostility to your own people. I've never understood it. You belong on our team."

"The hell I do."

He shook his head. "A friendly warning, Andy. You're giving the Bar too much credit. Don doesn't care shit about you. He's a bigot, through and through."

I laughed. "You're just jealous."

~

The next morning I dressed in a dark blue suit, similar to one Don had worn the day before, accessorized with my gold-tipped cane. I could envision wearing the ensemble again at my swearing-in ceremony.

I headed for the courtroom, but was stopped by a clerk at the door.

"Mr. Martin, Judge Clemons wants you in his chambers."

"Now?"

"Yes."

What was this about? Maybe López had pulled out. Still a win, but less satisfying, less notable.

The judge motioned me in. I smiled until I saw Bob Tettleman seated in one of the overstuffed chairs. I must have been right.

"Sit down, Andrew," Clemons said, tugging at his robe.

I glanced sideways at Bob, whose expression I couldn't read.

"You have a problem, Andy."

"I?"

"Josh Barker."

"What about him?"

"He's, uh, apparently had a twinge of conscience. Wants to recant, or rather, clarify his testimony."

"Meaning?" I said.

Clemons turned to Bob.

"Josh came to see me," Bob said.

"You?"

"Yeah. Wants to switch sides. Says Patterson lied, that López actually worked harder than Josh himself. That the money was for something else."

"What? I don't believe it. Your Guild must have gotten to him."

"I swear to you. He came of his own accord. Called me last night."

I looked from Clemons to Bob. They were serious. Fuck. Not like me to get blindsided. "What was the something else?"

"That's the most troubling part," Bob said. "Josh said he was paid to watch López, find something incriminating. Patterson wanted a reason to fire him."

"What?! Where's Josh?"

"Waiting for you, room three."

"Andy," Clemons said. "I've got to let him back on the stand."

~

It took thirty minutes, fifteen with Josh, who confirmed everything, and fifteen with Patterson, who was so stunned that he couldn't deny it. The only route left was to convince the jury that Josh's story wasn't credible. Count on their bias and hope that a few of them were jazz fans.

The courtroom was shocked by the turn of events. Bob presented it as a victory for truth, letting Josh tell his own story after being sworn back in. I cross-examined, a fruitless attempt to get Josh to implicate the Guild. In my closing, I questioned the timing of his sudden admission, regretting it, however, when Bob countered by saying that doing the right thing "didn't run on a schedule." That comment elicited a collective nod from jury, which, at noon, began deliberations.

An hour passed, and then another. By three they were still at it, so I went to Pershing Square for some fresh air. I threw the pigeons some cracker crumbs from my pocket. They were less than enthusiastic.

I didn't like how I was feeling. Furious at Patterson. A little sympathetic toward López. Topsy-turvy. An imbalance that also allowed that damn Salvationist, that unlucky Penny, to slip in.

Mostly though, I was thinking about what this would mean for my chances with the Bar. If it went against us, Patterson would only get a slap on the wrist, maybe a fine. But what about me?

Someone was approaching. The clerk. "Mr. Martin, they're back."

~

"Have you reached a verdict?"

"We have, your Honor. We find in favor of the plaintiff."

The courtroom exploded. The press scurried out. Patterson hung his head. Tettleman hugged his client. Clemons set the sentencing date for Thursday, glanced at me and frowned.

I told George that had I known about his scheme, I wouldn't have defended him, although I wasn't sure I'd meant it. My leg was tingling, and I almost wished for a flare-up, that it and the rest of me would disappear. The fans were disgruntled, and from the comments I could make out, more disappointed in me than in George. I eyed the exit, but halfway there I spotted Don, laughing with someone from the D.A.'s office. I slowed, waited, let a few people by. Finally I caught his gaze, but there was no reaction. Indeed, he looked right through me, as if I'd gotten my wish.

# 5

## MISSION

ATTORNEY ANDREW MARTIN MAY HAVE FINALLY LOST HIS MIDAS TOUCH, GOLD-TIPPED CANE AND ALL.

I flung the paper across the room, forcing Emerson to duck. He was getting better at it. This was the fifth article in as many days about the case—unusual for a civil matter—and he'd learned what to expect. It wasn't just that I'd lost, it was that a Mexican, other than myself, had won that made for ongoing headlines.

Not only that, but my phone had been silent. No new calls, no new cases. And no call from Don. Most maddening of all, I kept imagining Bob Tettleman saying that he told me so.

I'd been drinking. Today, much too early. As I'd predicted, the woman suing about the furniture dropped the case. But that was little comfort. Yesterday, George was fined a thousand dollars. No big deal for him financially, but a humiliation to us both. Plus, Penny. My mother. With time on my hands, I'd had a hard time keeping the lid on that box closed.

By the time I'd gotten home, it was near six, and I was sobering up. I could hold my liquor too well some would say. I did have my limits, though, and tonight was dinner at the Beatons. I needed something extra. Something to boost my confidence. Tonight I needed the Miltown.

I had only taken the tranquilizer twice before, once to try it, and the other, a few months ago, when the *Times* ran an article about farm workers that mentioned my father:

> *In all of our interviews, one name repeatedly came up, the late Carlos Martínez. These people revere him...would canonize him if they could....*

Few would have noticed the article, let alone care, and soon I didn't either because the pill had worked like a dream, blunting the adrenaline that ignited my symptoms. "Only when you absolutely must," the doctor had said. "Brand new." "Powerful." Must I, I'd asked myself, absolutely? Until now, the answer had usually been no. Booze was one thing. But there was something about a prescription that made me feel weak, as in my hospital days. Just now, however, I swallowed one down and lay on my bed until it kicked in.

I switched on the light, which got Emerson's attention. He was in tune with my moods and moped in his cage during the worst of them. The light meant I was better so he started fluttering around. "Andrew Martin, Esquire! Andrew Martin, Esquire!" I half-smiled. He landed on my shoulder and stayed there while I turned on the radio. My neighbors were going at it again. I wondered if this otherwise lethargic couple did much else. I twisted the knob to KUSC, the classical station housed at my alma mater, and upped the volume until the music, a Beethoven piano concerto, drowned out their moans.

The pill seemed to be working. My body felt loose, like a marionette, but at least now I was in control of the strings. I stood up. The carpet felt thicker than usual and the air smelled friendly. I was relaxed but not drowsy. I ordered Emerson to his corner perch. He flew away but returned when he heard me open my closet. He knew what that meant and faked a human cry to show his disapproval.

I ran my hand over the row of suits and dinner jackets. "Which one, boy?" That snapped him out of it. He liked to be included and gestured near the middle. "Yes," I said. "I think you're right." I removed the double-breasted, black sport coat from the hanger and smoothed it out. Add a grey shirt, I thought, and a silk handkerchief. Sedate enough for John, alluring enough for Cici.

I showered, dried off and listened at the wall for sounds. It was quiet, so I changed the station to jazz. Television? No, I didn't have one yet. I wasn't in a hurry to invite all those faces into my home. Better to stay in the darkened theater where they belonged. I slipped on my pants, which were fuller in the leg than the current trend. This was a personal preference, given my condition, and not a nod, as John often joked, to the Zoot suit.

The rest of the outfit fell into place and even Emerson peeped a reluctant approval. "Go!" I said, before leaving. He squawked and fluttered, but ultimately obeyed, recovering some cinnamon sticks from his favorite hiding place. I tugged open my pocket, and he dropped them in, one by one.

~

The Beatons lived in a Grecian-themed mansion. Pillars, urns, even a statue of Aphrodite. Marble from floor to ceiling. The neighborhood was Bel Air, the most exclusive in L.A., but that didn't make their home any less tasteless.

"May I take your coat, sir?"

"Thank you," I said to Ed, the butler who appeared as amused as I was with his exaggerated bow. He was new to the scene, an obstacle that would have to be overcome if things with Cici remained as they were.

I waited in the foyer. I could see the winding staircase that led to the bedrooms. I smiled to myself, thinking of how intimately I knew the one at the end of the hall. The feel of the satin, the slight sag of the mattress. We'd managed to evade the maid and the cook, but Ed would be a challenge. Perhaps this was a sign that I had finally exceeded my welcome.

On the wall directly in front of me hung a new painting. It, too, had a Greek subject: Poseidon, with his beard, trident and all. It was garish, no doubt overpriced, a sign of status rather than quality.

"Like it?" John said, suddenly beside me.

"John," I said, pretending to admire the monstrosity. "How long have you had it?"

"A month. One of Cici's purchases."

"Of course I do."

John winked, although I doubted he understood my tone.

"You've got quite a tan," I said.

"We've been in Palm Springs. Wait until you see Cici. She could pass for your sister."

"Can't wait."

"Come on. Let me get you a drink."

I followed him into the den. John was a large man, bald and broad, with a heavy, confident walk. He was his own animal, a hybrid species. From the back, a bear, from the front, a reptile. He was only fifty, but was frequently mistaken for older because of his love of the sun. Yet he was striking, with quick, silvery eyes.

He handed me a rum. I was a little wary of adding another round to the mix, but it went down fine.

"Read about the trial," John said.

"Yeah."

"Patterson's an idiot."

"Wish I'd known that ahead of time."

"You didn't ask me."

I shrugged.

"How's business, otherwise?" he said.

"Can't complain."

"Still on our side?"

"I'm on *my* side," I said.

"Ha! That's why I like you, Andy. No bullshit. Tell me," he said, lowering his voice, "any cases that couldn't be postponed for a month? Or handed off to someone else?"

"Why, what's on your mind?"

"After dinner," he said, checking his watch. "I've got to make a call. Stay here for a minute, will you?"

I nodded, feeling curious. Did he want me to represent him again? If so, it would have to be a big case, one that required my full attention. But why so mysterious? I was considering the possibilities when I smelled Cici. Her musky perfume always preceded her.

"Hello," she said.

I turned to the doorway, where she stood, golden-skinned, cocktail in hand. A fine vintage, tall and svelte with the cheekbones of a model. Thirty-eight in a much younger body. Tonight she wore a long emerald-green tunic, and she'd twisted her dyed red hair into a high bun.

"Haven't seen you in a while," she said, slithering toward me.

"Whose fault is that?"

She got close and pecked my cheek. "Yours."

I smirked. A one-night stand had somehow stretched into a year. That's what it was with Cici. Absolutely nothing would come of it, and I'd told her so. She'd agreed to the terms and thus far had stuck to them. But I feared that sooner or later she'd let something slip. And even before tonight, I had started to feel guilty. John had been good to me, and I'd returned the favor by sleeping with his wife. Just like my father had done to all those poor saps, the one sleazy part of him I'd been unable to shed. At least that's what I'd always thought. Perhaps, I'd inherited the trait from my mother. Perhaps I was doomed from the start.

~

"Now," John said, returning to the den.

Cici retracted, pretending to rearrange the roses on the coffee table. This was the one room in the house that possessed some class, even if it wasn't my style. Dark wood, old books and only one nod to Greece, a black and white photograph of contemporary Athens. And yet, I felt the sneaking presence of a Trojan horse.

John nuzzled Cici's neck as she stood fiddling. "What did I tell, you, Andy? Wouldn't she blend in on Olvera Street?"

"John, you're awful," Cici said, batting him away.

"Yes, you are, John. You're lucky I have a sense of humor. And, really, your joke doesn't even work. Olvera attracts your people, not mine."

~

"Come," John said, "let's sit down."

The table had been shortened to accommodate the three of us. It usually spanned the full length of the dining room, with all the leaves in to give it a grand impression. It was easier to converse this way, but the new version was dwarfed in the palatial space. It, and I, felt imbalanced.

The meal helped to restore my equilibrium. Hilda, a sturdy

Norwegian, was an excellent cook, and tonight she'd outdone herself with a rack of lamb and homemade mint jelly. Wine flowed, and John kept the conversation on politics. We discussed Frank Reed's loss in the mayoral primary and agreed that the reelection of Fletcher Bowron wasn't such a bad thing. He'd done a lot for the infrastructure of the city and had somewhat cleaned up City Hall. Yes, he'd been in favor of the internment camps, but nobody's perfect. He'd regretted his position, and at least there was still a Republican at the helm.

With dinner done, however, I grew weary of waiting for whatever had brought me here. Cici kept giving me looks. After the wine, John offered some Black Label and a rare cognac. I declined. I wanted to go home. I pushed my chair back, signaling my desire to leave.

John sprang up from his chair. "Andy! No, no. Time got away from me. You must stay. Cici, dear, would you mind? We've got some business to discuss."

She stood. "Stay seated, gentlemen." She smiled at John and, almost imperceptibly, pouted at me. "Good night."

~

"Andrew," John said. "First, what I'm about to tell you is confidential."

I nodded, for whatever that was worth.

John got up and paced the room, running his fingers through his non-existent hair. "Okay, I'll get right to the point. You're aware that some top Nazis escaped to South America after the war."

"Yeah, I've heard that."

"Are you also aware that some got out before the war was over?"

I sighed, with intentional annoyance.

"And do you know that some went to other countries?"

"John, I'm not in the mood for twenty questions."

"All right," John said, lowering his voice. "How's this? There are ex-Nazis living in California; invited *by* and working *for* the U.S. government. They're part of an undercover project called Operation Paperclip."

"Okay," I said.

"*Okay*? That's all you have to say? You're not outraged?"

"I suppose if I think about it."

John exhaled. "The Pentagon, FBI and CIA have each provided sanctuary for these criminals in exchange for information. War plans, scientific data. They use these agents to spy on the Soviets and communists living here. They've been doing it for years."

I chewed on a stick. I'd heard hints of such a practice, but never thought much about it. Frank Reed, when he was state senator and member of the House Un-American Activities Committee, had never mentioned it, although maybe he wouldn't. I was only an acquaintance, a one-time supporter but not part of his inner circle. But what was John getting at? How did he know this? And most importantly, why had he told me?

Before I could ask, John added: "I have information that one of these fiends is living in Sacramento. One of the worst. A doctor, like Mengele."

I laughed a little. "What kind of game is this?"

"No game, I promise you."

"All right," I said. "No game. But..."

"Why should you care?"

"Well, yes, I mean, if it's true as you say, it's concerning. Of course, I would care, as any other citizen would. But what does this have to do with me, personally?"

"I thought you were a patriot."

"You'll need to do better than that."

John sat down and poured himself another cognac. His bald head gleamed with sweat. "I've never told you. Very few people know, in fact," he said, swirling his drink. "My mother. My mother was Jewish."

I almost laughed again. But he gazed at me with such intensity that I knew he wasn't kidding. John? Jewish? "Really?" I pictured him with a beanie. *Yarmulke, Mr. Martin.*

"Yes. I was raised Protestant, like my father. But my mother, who died when I was eleven, was a Jew. And as I've gotten older, with the war and all, I've begun to think about it. More and more. You know, in the Jewish religion, if your mother is a Jew, then you're a Jew."

*If your mother is a whore, then you're...*

"Andy," he continued. "I've gotten involved in an organization, a group dedicated to exposing these bastards. A few of the members were in the camps."

"Really?" I said again, finding this news almost more surprising. It was hard to think of John, captain of industry, moderately intolerant, dedicating himself to such a humanitarian cause, no matter what the connection. "And how will you expose them? I mean, if they're employed by the government, what's your goal?"

"Well, I've never been a fan of Truman. Did you know his wife Bess won't even allow Jews in their home? That's tolerance for you. I wouldn't mind this coming to light on strictly partisan grounds. Anti-Semitism isn't restricted to country clubs and hotels, you know. It's everywhere. That's one of the reasons I'm glad Frank didn't make it in the primary. You must have heard him crack jokes about Jews being cheap. And worse."

I had.

"Even medical schools have quotas. Even after Hitler. Think of Roosevelt, who turned away all those Jewish refugees from

Germany. Democrats are as bad as, maybe even worse than, Republicans."

He was right, I supposed, although most Jews I knew were Democrats. I hadn't much thought of it. I was a Republican for other reasons—individualistic, financial, because my father was the opposite. Growing up in Boyle Heights, I'd known Jewish kids. Kids like David, the paper boy. But as a Mexican, I'd had enough to worry about.

"Still," he continued, "we believe that Americans need to know who's living in their county. Maybe next door to them. Jews are one thing. Nazis quite another. Our goal is the press, Andy. An article, exposé. We'll let the cards fall where they may after that."

"This is all fascinating," I said. "But I'm at a loss. What do you want from me?"

"We want to hire you."

"Me? Hire me to do what? This isn't my line."

John slowly looked up. His expression gave me a start. It was neither bird nor bear. Something new. A third element. I examined his features. He was the same man, and yet he wasn't. All that time working with him, and not a hint. But, strangely, I felt more sympathetic, as if he were a long-lost relative, someone, who, like me, was not exactly what he appeared.

"I didn't say it was your line, Andy. But it just may be your destiny. Our organization needs someone like you. We need to know our rights. How far we can go."

"With what?"

"With whatever comes up. We don't want to break the law, but we may need to stretch it. We need a lawyer's knowledge. Mostly, however, we need your detective's sensibility. We *believe* the man in Sacramento is our Mengele. But your, shall we say, talent for discovery, even for a little acting, can help us be certain.

"Acting?"

"You know, like you did with the IAM situation. Damn genius you were with that one."

I felt a momentary pleasant rush. In '46, John had heard rumors that the IAM, the machinists union, was planning to strike. They wanted more money, and most of his employees were union members. During the war, plane parts were in high demand. Business was booming. He could afford to pay top dollar. But orders had slowed, and he'd had to cut wages. The men weren't happy, but he'd had no choice. That is, if he wanted to maintain his own lavish lifestyle.

So he called me. Not to act as his lawyer, but to do a little snooping. He knew there was no love lost between me and the unions. Also, that I had a knack for gaining sympathy and trust. After all, by then juries had handed me far more wins than losses. The idea appealed to me. I'd always liked the investigative part of my job, and this would be an extension of that. I'd have to be careful, of course, but my only real concern was that someone might recognize me. That Mexican lawyer with the walking stick. The one with the American name. The son of a legend. So I disguised myself, wore coveralls and eyeglasses. My stint in local theater, which I'd given up after 4-F, had finally come in handy. I covered my head with a wide-brimmed hat, traded the cane for a walker, and made a habit of visiting the employee gathering spot. Within two weeks, I'd learned the terms and proposed date of the strike, details that were later confirmed. The union backed down, and John had been so pleased with my work that he hired me to snoop again. Only this time it was more personal. This time he wanted me to tail Cici, whom he thought might be having an affair. I took that job, too, and delivered him positive news, that his fears were unfounded. What I didn't say was that I didn't know how long that would remain the case.

"Why not hire someone up there?" I said.

"Well, for one thing, your experience. The suspect attends labor union meetings, if you can believe that irony. Government must think that's a clever way to root out a Red. But with you on board, it might be an even cleverer way to root out a Nazi."

"Huh."

John grabbed my hand and held it up, as if we were going to arm wrestle. "More than anything though, Andy, I know you. Respect you. Trust you. As much as I would a son."

I flushed and pulled away.

"There'd be money in it."

Money I had. But... "I'll need to mull it over," I said.

He stood up. "When you're mulling, remember."

"Remember what?"

His eyes fixed on me, and not in a fatherly way. I couldn't read them. I glanced at the photograph of Greece, the blanched dwellings, the tranquil sea and white sand.

"The war. The draft. You have unfinished business with the country, Andy. Come on. I knew what day it was when I invited you over."

What *day* it was? What day...?

"Andy?"

I didn't answer.

"Andy."

"I can't believe you remember the date," I said, feeling almost warmth toward the man.

He smiled. "I've always been good with numbers."

~

I turned onto Wilshire, where a late showing of *Battleground* at the El Rey appeared to be just getting out. A crowd mingled as the red marquee lights flickered off. Nearby, a motorcycle cop was writing up some unfortunate driver. I would have to watch myself.

I rolled down the car window and let the night air blow in. It stung a little, but it also brought me around. John, a Jew? Tracking down Nazis? That dining room must have been low on oxygen, or maybe it was the Miltown. Was my need for redemption so great that I could suspend all disbelief? Had I forgotten that I was a mere token, not only John's favorite, but *only* Mexican friend? I knew him, but how well, really? He certainly didn't know everything about me. Maybe he *had* found out about Cici. Maybe he was trying to set me up. Maybe his story was only partially true, or, as could be the case with even the most credible of witnesses, entirely fabricated.

I'd think about it all right. But before that, I'd have to do some checking. Verify every detail. Make sure I wasn't being played. Destiny was for the gullible, for astrologers and lovers. If it had anything to do with me, I'd have to be damn sure that my stars had hard facts behind their alignment.

I started down the sidewalk to my apartment, limping a little again. Under the outdoor lamp, the soupy air swirled yellow. I sniffed, flaring my nostrils to accommodate all the smells: eucalyptus, skunk, grass, concrete, salt, garbage.

And then I caught a whiff of something else, something earthly and familiar. "Christ! I said. "What the hell are you doing here?"

Standing near my door in the full-length, gossamer gown—the one I'd buried my face in, the one I'd lifted and tugged and even once slightly tore—hands curved on her hourglass hips, was Cici.

"I wouldn't have to freeze out here if you'd just given me a key," she said.

"How did you get here?"

"The usual way."

"You know what I mean. Isn't John going to notice?"

"You know we don't sleep together."

"He could knock on your door, want to kiss you goodnight."

"He knows better. Besides, it's locked."

"All right, but how?"

"You were still talking when I went up to bed. I called a cab, went down the back stairs, had him pick me up on the corner. *Voila!*"

Cici. I shook my head. I should have told her to leave. But I was already aroused, already wanted her. She could make me forget about everything, subdue my overcharged senses. I might very well disappear, but there would be no pain. And I'd be guaranteed a swift return.

This would be the last time, I vowed.

# 6

## DRAFTED

The next day was hot, dry and windy. Indian summer. Everyone had been waiting for it. To some, a symbol of second chances. To others, an imitation. To me, a memory. Sitting on the curb, barefoot. Hair blowing every which way, eyes swollen from crying. A neighborhood kid asking how my mother died. Me not answering, feeling sad, empty, lost. As I did just now, except with a caveat: *your mother is alive*. Emerson must have felt the same because he hadn't yet left his cage. Or he might have been punishing me, as he often did when Cici had been there.

The first thing I did after washing the sheets and airing out the room was swear on my dog-eared copy of *Moby Dick* that the affair was over. I told Cici as much while she was getting dressed. I was gentle about it, using my guilt as the reason why I simply couldn't deceive John anymore. She chuckled at first and started to undress again, trying then and there to prove me wrong. But after I didn't react, she realized I was serious. Or at least she went through the motions. Meaning I don't think she really believed me. She left abruptly with a hurt expression, but I didn't buy it. Her step out the door had too much of a bounce.

I called John before leaving for work to tell him that I needed a week to look into his offer. I said: "No one in his right mind would agree without confirming the facts."

"Of course," John said, "I understand. Take your week."

Emerson finally peeked out of his cage.

"You won't have to deal with her anymore," I said, holding out my finger. He jumped on, bobbing his head happily, as if he knew what I meant.

"Andrew Martin, Esquire! Andrew Martin, Esquire!"

Yes, Esquire, I thought, and I'm going to use that title to pull some strings. Talk to Louise at Vital Records. She owes me a favor. Frank Reed. Need to see him, too.

I heard the newspaper slap the front porch. "Hey, Dave," I said, out the window, "Emerson's losing weight. Hasn't had any of your treats in a while."

Dave looked up but remained on his bike. "My parents don't want me going into my customers' houses anymore."

"Oh? Why is that?"

He glanced around and rode up closer. "A guy on the route yelled at me."

"Late delivery?"

He balanced on his pedals, making the bike quiver. "He said I'd make a good lampshade."

"What?"

"I didn't understand what he meant, but my mom told me."

I eyed one of my own lamps and felt queasy. "That's awful, David. Do you know who he was?"

"No. He ran away. I don't think he was actually one of my customers. He was on the sidewalk, across the street. But my parents said better to be safe than sorry."

"I see."

Emerson fluttered around near the cabinet where I kept the seed.

"Okay, boy," I said.

"I'll sneak some more cracker when I can, Mr. Martin. I sure miss feeding the little guy."

"Well, I don't want you to get into trouble. Do what your parents say."

~

I scanned the headlines as Emerson ate, almost disappointed that the press had finally tired of me:

CHINA REDS RACE TO TRAP CANTON ARMY; FORMER DEMOCRATIC SENATOR AND NEW DEALER SHERMAN MINTON TOOK OATH AS A JUSTICE OF THE SUPREME COURT TODAY IN A WHITE HOUSE CEREMONY; DAVE OGUL, 30, CHAUFFER AND BODYGUARD OF MOBSTER MICKEY COHEN WAS REPORTED MISSING LAST NIGHT.

Emerson pecked down his food, and on his own, retrieved my sticks. He was indeed in a very good mood. "Esquire! Esquire!"

"I know," I said. "I know."

~

October twenty-sixth. A week since Indian summer had begun and still no sign of retreat. The sultry wind brought with it an almost nauseating sweetness, like the smell of rotting flowers. If I was melancholic at the onset, I was downright depressed now. One can only live with an imitation for so long.

I sat at my desk waiting for Frank Reed. My research into John's offer had ground to a halt a few days ago after a pipe burst in my apartment, water flooding the kitchen. My furniture was saved, but I had to move into the vacant studio next door for three nights, a furnished but cramped space in which neither Emerson nor I could sleep. Now, time was of the essence.

I told Frank I'd heard he was thinking about running for something again and wondered, even though I knew he had no chance, if he needed any advice. He was receptive. He'd already hired a lawyer, he said, but he did want to ask me something and offered to meet me at my office. And Louise. I was waiting to hear from her, too. She'd discovered that John was telling the truth about his father having a second wife, but, as of yet, nothing else. However, she'd called earlier and left a message with my answering service. I'd called back, but she was in a meeting.

I chewed on a stick and went to the window. The wind had dusted the buildings clean but was swirling wrappers and other bits of trash on the sidewalk. A couple of large palm fronds lay splattered on the street. The surreal blue sky lent to the mountains such clarity that I could almost see individual trees thirty miles away. What peace. If only I could bottle it.

My leg had been stable, but my mind was in turmoil, weighing John's offer. Even if everything checked out, where exactly would I be staying? Who would I report to? *Andrew Martin, Esquire*! Okay, but being a lawyer might not be enough. The duties were still vague. And yet....

The buzzer rang. Even if it hadn't, though, I'd have known Frank by the odor of his cigar. It wasn't woody or sweet or even like burning grass. It was uniquely acrid.

"Andy. *Amigo*!"

I cringed, but held it in. "Frank. It's been a while. Sit down."

Frank was fair and pudgy with a pitted alkie's nose. His cloudy eyes masked his ambition.

"I was glad to hear from you, Andy. I know we have our differences."

"Yes. So what are you going for this time?"

"Mayor again. Thought I might soften the tone, you know. Try to reach out."

"What did you want to ask me?"

"Well, I thought you might be of some help in the barrios."

"Really? Come on. You know my people don't trust me."

"Yeah, your father, I know, but maybe, if you told them that Hearst would support me..."

I wanted to wring his neck. What did he know about my father? That I had disowned him? Everyone knew that. That he was a unionizer, agitator, died for the cause? Ditto. Surface, all surface.

"Hearst? That's not going to help. He's a bigot. You need someone like Earl Warren, someone who actually accepts that you don't have to be white to be human."

"But Governor Warren's not a *real* Republican."

Meaning he thought for himself. Was his own man. "I'll do what I can."

"That's all I ask."

"I appreciate your willingness to help, Andy, really I do. And you know, I never really thought of myself as a Red baiter, just a loyal American."

Right. I guessed the Guild wasn't all bad. They'd defended, still were defending, the Hollywood crowd against Reed and his cronies. I was a Republican, but this right-wing hunt for communists had become a travesty. Gone way too far, to the point, if John was right, that they'd enlisted Nazis as bloodhounds.

"I know. You're a patriot."

"Exactly."

I thought of Hearst. Hard to believe he was once for

Roosevelt. Like a typical convert, he'd zealously embraced what he'd once hated. Even interviewed Hitler for one of his yellow rags, something Frank probably cheered. Warren was different. He was conservative, but tolerant. Bent toward the left in terms of human rights. Except, of course, where the Japanese were concerned, since he was the architect of the internment camps.

"Oh, that reminds me," I said. "I've heard this rumor, well, it's ridiculous, of course, about Nazis spying for the government. Spying on Reds. Know anything about that?"

Frank was about to take a drag on his cigar. He opened his lips, preparing to receive the fat stogie. But the action stopped mid-stream. For a moment, he was motionless, except for his eyes. He scanned the room, appearing to search for a response.

Finally, he let out a short laugh. "Ridiculous is right."

"So, it's not true?" I said.

He lit the cigar. "Who'd you hear that from, anyway?"

"I don't even remember."

"Well, I wouldn't waste my time on it."

"I won't. Just curious."

The phone rang. Maybe it was Louise. "Frank, I need to take this."

"I'll wait."

I didn't want him to, but I let him stay.

"Andrew Martin."

"Please don't hang up, Mr. Martin,"

"Louise?"

"Penny. Penny Crane."

"Miss Crane," I gritted out.

"Mr. Martin. I'm just wondering. Have you by chance reconsidered? Your mother is..."

Frank was smoking, watching me. "Just a minute," I said to Penny.

"Frank, could we talk later? This is about a case. I'll be a while."

He frowned but got up. "Next week," he said.

I nodded.

At the door he turned: "And don't bother with that Nazi business."

I waited for the door to shut and counted to ten. "No. I have not reconsidered. Nor will I," I said, and hung up.

I felt cold. My leg tingled a little. Home. I wanted to go home.

But home to what? My bird, of course. Emerson, poor thing. A creature of the jungle whose ability to survive there had been domesticated out of him. A weakened being. All talk, like his owner. Yes, I'd go home to my bird. My home. A modernly furnished cage where I was imprisoned by a calendar, by the next anniversary, and the next.

I called Louise again. She was in, and she had news.

"It does appear that his mother was Jewish," she said. "We found a birth certificate. John Clarence Beaton, born to Sophie Feuerstein Beaton. August 25, 1892. Sophie Feuerstein's records, too. Daughter of a clothing manufacturer in Manhattan. Died from TB in 1908. Oh, and regarding that other person you wanted to know about, Isabella Martínez. No. No death certificate in that time frame."

I sat back, took it all in. I thought of David. The end of the war certainly hadn't ended the hatred. I thought about the German people, too, how so many of them pled ignorance about the Final Solution. There were still the questions, of course, logistical, existential. But Louise, and without intending to, Frank, lent credibility to John's story. Telling me to drop it. Twice. Maybe that shouldn't have been enough. Maybe I was looking for an escape. But I'd lost the Patterson case, and along with it, my chance at the big time. Cici was over. I needed to keep it that way. And Penny.

She wouldn't stop, unless there was no way to reach me. So maybe it wasn't enough, but it would have to be. I'd been called up, and this time I was 1A.

# 8

## BOOT CAMP

Emerson had stayed at Martha's before, but he knew something was different. The two suitcases were a giveaway. He had watched as I packed: first curious, then sullen, and finally dejected. He went limp when I put him in the cage, which was almost worse than throwing a fit, like the time he dive-bombed my head for locking him out of the bedroom.

I was glad that Martha, aka the Bird Lady, had taken a liking to him. At any one time she housed some thirty-odd birds in her run-down Pasadena craftsman. She looked part bird herself and treated all these flying orphans as her children. Her place was a mess, devoid of human comforts, and I wondered about the legality of Martha's permit. But there was love in that home. For the wounded, the sick, the lonely. I sat in my car for a minute, observing Martha through her bay window. Emerson was resting on her right shoulder, and as I backed out of her driveway, I wondered what it would feel like to sit on her left.

~

It was December 7th. Winter. If not quite by the calendar. I headed north along the Arroyo Seco, the seasonal river and canyon region that just now was anything but *seco*. Cooler temperatures had finally arrived and with them heavy rain, the kind that threatened floods and mudslides. Thick overcast had dulled the area's usually vivid greens. Palms were scarce in this part of town, and many of the native trees—sycamore, ash, walnut—were leafless.

Two months had passed, and I was finally on my way to Sacramento. I'd had to wrap things up at the office, but the delay had mostly been the result of the suspect, the Nazi turned American spy, suddenly disappearing. John's colleagues initially feared that he'd left for good, but he'd recently returned with a truck full of baby furniture, a Christmas tree, and a wife about to give birth. That suggested he'd be around for a while, and I was beginning to feel actual enthusiasm for the job. The clincher was a report John had given me about the difference between how Jews and Nazis were treated by the U.S. after the war. In short, that Jews were often denied immigration, left in the camps to rot, while Nazis were "cleansed" of their pasts and provided U.S. citizenship. Their skills were just too alluring, as was their hatred of all things Russian. Never mind that they were murderers. Root out some commies and call it good. When I let that injustice sink it, I was even more certain that I'd made the right decision.

*What about your own, people, Mijo? What about the injustices to them? The whitewashing of their culture, the stealing of their land. The every day humiliations. Not grand enough for you?*

That's what my father would have said. But I turned him off, as one would an endlessly repeating record. I could choose my injustice. There was enough to go around.

It had also been two months since I'd seen Cici. I'd heard from her, though. Once, twice, sometimes three times a day.

Nothing had deterred her, and I'd feared an escalation. Until a week ago, when the calls abruptly stopped. Perhaps because she knew I was leaving. John had told her that I would be traveling for him on business, although not in what capacity. Perhaps she had met someone else, taken my advice to move on. Whatever the reason, I was cautiously relieved.

A fine mist covered the windshield. I'd had the car overhauled before leaving and that included a new set of wipers. I switched them on and marveled at their efficiency. Mist turned to drops as I merged onto the 99, the long stretch of highway that I would travel for the next five days. I planned to arrive December 12th. That's when the welcoming committee, as John put it, would be expecting me. I could have flown, left later in the week, but I thought a trip on the road might do me some good. An unhurried pace, a slow rehearsal before the big show. Besides, December 7th had a certain ring to it.

Bakersfield, my first planned overnight, was about a hundred miles north. I'd been to Paris and Rome, but nowhere between San Francisco and L.A. Strange, I know, but there had never been a reason, and I hadn't missed anything. Flat and dry, irrigation pipes and oil wells. Nothing to inflame my senses. Nothing but the rain, that is, which had suddenly come into its own. Even with the wipers, I strained a bit to see. A few headlights, highway signs, billboards. I sat to attention and tried to fix my gaze on the road. But that rain. It reminded me of... I gripped the wheel, felt my foot on the gas. The car was moving forward, but I was traveling back to Boyle Heights.

~

*I'm six or seven, running from room to room. I draw the curtains shut, hold my ears against the terrible noise.*

*"Mijo," my father says. "It's rain, only rain. Come here."*

*He's sitting on the couch, pointing to the window. "See?" he says.*

*Yes, I see! Arrows, pelting the windows! I rush to his side, trying to avoid a hit. I nuzzle his broad chest, contract my body, try to merge with his.*

~

A horn honked.

I jumped. "Yeah, yeah!" I said, checking my speed. I had slowed to 40 mph. The car passed and honked again for emphasis.

Mijo, that's what he used to call me. And Pop is what I called him. I could almost smell the oranges. They lingered on his skin, the bitter pith he munched like chocolate. Pop. It was hard to believe that at one time I'd felt safe with him. As safe as Emerson with Martha.

I swallowed the lump in my throat and checked the map, not out of need, but for comfort. Lines and swirls. Numbers and names. A reassuring document to keep me on track.

A long incline lay ahead. The Tejon Pass, reaching an elevation of four thousand feet. Fortunately it wasn't cold enough to snow. I hadn't brought any chains. All I'd taken were my suitcases, which were in the trunk, and a small, canvas bag, sitting in the passenger seat. It held the essentials: my camera—a barely used Leica Rangefinder—a supply of sticks, a flask of rum and the Miltown.

I continued up and up, the car grunting like an old man. Steep, muddy hillsides sprang up on either side of the road, which made me feel something between protected and hemmed in. Ahead lay sodden grasses and trees, some with leaves, some without. Rain-soaked shrubs as far as the eye could see. Wiry, white branches, jangling in the wind. Round, fat bushes, seemingly equidistant. A patchwork of tangled skeletons and bushy ogres that looked capable of evil.

Not very many cars, so I tried to accelerate. The engine's stiff joints creaked forward. Still, driving in these conditions was dicey, so I held the steering wheel with both hands and checked my mirrors frequently.

Finally I reached the summit. The terrain had changed, the patchwork given way to barren, velvety rolling hills. The hills struck me as opaque drapery folds, hiding whatever was over the ridge.

Like the welcoming committee. Who were they? John said a few had been in those trains, were camp survivors, with the tattoos to prove it. To them, the fact that Nazis had set foot in this country was bad enough. But that they'd done so at the behest of the U.S. government was a betrayal worse than even that of their hero, Roosevelt, turning away those boatloads of refugees because they could have been Nazi spies.

*Jews. Don't trust them, Mijo. All they care about is money.*

That's right. Pop, too, had an anti-Semitic strain, although it softened after he met the woman he called the Jewess. Sarah. How could I forget? The woman he was seeing before he was killed. He made excuses for her, said she was one of the good ones. I'd met her once. And she seemed good. A good person, that is. Better than most of his broads. For all his liberalism, my father had his blind spots. Said the Jewish grocers he dealt with were cheats, the Jews in our Boyle Heights neighborhood snobs, although when I asked him to explain, he couldn't. Strange, too, since Jews often rallied to his causes.

I started to descend. My ears cracked, the vista expanded. Before me a wide, flat valley. I stretched as much of my body as I could without crashing, but also my mind, imagining the committee, stereotypically, as my father might have, as bearded men in Hassidic garb. Why, I'm not sure, except that they are the most identifiable of Jews. Maybe also because David once told me about his Hassidic relatives who worked in the jewelry district. Even in summer, dressed in black, head to toe. Heavy coats, high hats, their long sideburns twisted and curled. Identifiable and miserable, I'd always thought, suffering the heat, afraid to embrace modernity. Until one day, when I'd walked by one of their stores after closing. I could hear music. The blinds were drawn, but the door was cracked open. I peaked in. Before me, a family, maybe two. Several children. A record was playing. Singing and dancing. They looked happy. I watched for a minute, envious, and took my time getting home.

I squinted at a sign up ahead. CALIFORNIA HISTORICAL LANDMARK. It was still raining, but I pulled over at the turnout to see what it was. Why not? I had time.

PEDRO FAGES. SPANISH EXPLORER. FIRST LIEUTENANT GOVERNOR SECOND AND FIFTH GOVERNOR OF ALTA CALIFORNIA. LED AN EXPEDITION IN 1772 THROUGH THIS PASS ON HIS WAY TO MONTEREY FROM SAN DIEGO.

*Strong, Mijo. Your people were strong. Pico, Arguello, Olvera. All the Californios. L.A. was settled by them. Your grandfather fought for them. Fought and died for the land that belonged to them. Always remember that. Keep the torch burning. Be proud!*

I turned off the engine but wasn't as successful at silencing my father. Sometimes he demanded entry, breaking through time as well as space. I watched the drops glide down the windshield.

Without the wipers to whisk them away, they appeared heavy and somber, like a giant's tears.

# 9

## BIVOUAC

The elevation dropped, the road leveled out. I felt a kind of mixed relief, glad for the open space but lonely at the sight of it. KERN COUNTY. Overgrown vines on either side of the road. There was a rest stop ahead. FOOD. GAS. I needed both. I turned off at the muddy exit and followed the arrow to a two-story shack with a single gas pump out front.

A squat, pasty woman with cotton-candy hair greeted me with an umbrella. She was wearing a flowered housedress, the kind my grandmother used to live in.

"*Hola. ¿Cómo estás?*" she said.

"Afternoon."

"Oh, you don't speak Spanish?"

"Afraid not," I said.

"I'm Audrey," she said, extending her nail-bitten hand. "Hungry?"

I was. And I had to piss. I followed her into a cheerless room with two wooden tables and a Formica counter. I shook off drops and stomped my feet on a rubber mat.

"Menu is on the board. BLT is our specialty, though."

"Okay. I'll have that. And a soda."

She gave the order to someone I couldn't see and hovered nearby. "Bathroom?" I said.

"In the back."

The toilet gurgled more than flushed. The sink had seen better days, too. The soap, however, was new, a fresh bar of Ivory. Snow white, devoid of film or even a strand of hair. I started to reach for it, but pulled back when I remembered that Ivory was the hospital's brand, what they made me wash myself with the day my father had me committed. The day he took off his mask and became a stranger. *Mijo, you need help. I'm sorry.*

Sorry. Sorry for what? Putting me in the loony bin or lying to me all my life? I wonder what he'd say now.

"Food is almost ready," Audrey said from the counter as soon as I came out.

I hadn't noticed the darkened jukebox, or the postcard display that appeared as if it had been there since the turn of the century. Nor the hankies, sunglasses, rabbits' feet and other good luck trinkets with yellowed price tags. An apparent attempt to brighten the area with dated holiday tinsel only exaggerated the sad effect. Unused. Stilled. The original purpose forgotten. Antiques without charm.

Even the guns in a rack on the sidewall seemed to have prematurely grown old. Ten or so. Rifles and pistols. I knew how to shoot—my father had taught me so that I could protect myself in an emergency. Still, I don't possess a weapon of my own. Truth is, I don't trust that sometime in a dark mood, I wouldn't mistake the mailman for an intruder. But who knew what I might encounter now?

"Are any of those for sale?" I said.

"Could be."

"Could?"

"Depends on which one."

"How about that small revolver," I said.

"Twenty bucks. Twenty-five with ammo. I always keep some around."

That seemed reasonable, and purchasing it buoyed me, almost as much as knowing the Miltown was only a cap twist away.

The sandwich was filling. I felt weighted down, as if my body were bolted to the ground. Even my leg. Audrey had extracted my occupation out of me and had "a million questions" about a squatter on the border of the property. The old man slept in his car and was usually gone by morning. But he claimed an inherited title to the land. Audrey doubted his story and had notified the cops. Or cop, because there was really only one in the region, and he was never around when the squatter was. She wanted to complain to someone, but the officials who oversaw her community were fifty miles away.

I told her that squatters' rights were complicated even in L.A., often wending through the system at a snail's pace. But, if this man was only there at night, why was she so bothered?

That's when the cook, her husband, Kip, lumbered out from the kitchen. Big and burly, tanned like leather with a patch over his left eye. He'd clearly been listening. "You mean other than him being a Jap?"

I met his venomous, one-eyed gaze. "Is there another reason, beside him being Japanese?"

Kip glanced at the empty tables. "I'll show you," he said, tossing his apron on the floor.

I followed him, gun in pocket, through a thicket of weeds to an open field. In the distance was a flock of sheep. Rain was spitting but Kip didn't seem to notice. A chain link fence separated what he said was their property from the squatter's. There was no trash, no sign of disruption.

He led me along the fence to a large tree whose wet, bare branches spilled over onto Kip's side of the fence. "There," he said, pointing to a black canvas tarp strung up like a lean-to, anchored with a couple of sticks. "See that thing there, whatever it is?"

I did see. Under the tarp. A marble Buddha. I crawled closer, muddying my hands as well as my pants. Next to the statue was a stone marker, engraved in English but I couldn't make it out. And incense. And what looked like an urn. This was a shrine. A grave.

I inadvertently bowed my head. "Have you ever asked him about it?" I said.

"Yeah. His son's ashes, so he says. Says the kid died in one of them camps. Got sick and died. Every goddamn night he lights that stuff and wails. We can hear him all the way from our place. He said the kid got TB. Ha. Those camps were clean, better than their homes, you can be sure."

"Why would he lie?"

The shrine reminded me of my grandmother's alter for the Virgin. Lovingly tended. The tarp, like my grandmother's bedroom, protecting it from the elements. His son.

"I'm tempted to burn it," Kip said.

"I'd just leave him alone if I were you," I said.

"But that property ain't his!"

"You don't know that. And, as a lawyer, I'm telling you it would be almost impossible to prove."

He didn't respond, just trudged back to the restaurant with furrowed brows.

A family had arrived in our absence. A salt-of-the-earth brood in matching Frosty the Snowman shirts. The parents were trying to corral their three children, who were chasing each other around the room.

Kip grunted and returned to the kitchen.

I accepted a to-go cup of coffee and returned their "Merry

Christmas" with a "same to you." The couple left me with a bad taste, and I felt lucky to make my escape. As soon as I got out of view, I stopped, tossed the coffee and retrieved a sweater and socks from the suitcase. My shoes were soaked, so I laid them in the back and slipped on my oxfords. Then I drove off, thinking of that shrine, the beauty of the thing, hoping that I'd done the squatter some good.

# 10

## NEAR MISS

I bolted up, hearing myself shriek. I darted my eyes around. Table, chair. Lamp, mirror. Motel. The Bakersfield Inn. Second floor. I checked my leg and fell back onto the bed. Sweat dripped down my bare chest. "Christ." I immediately thought of Cici, which meant that the nightmare surely had something to do with her. I must not have been as done with her as I thought.

I have a lot of nightmares. Not surprising, I suppose. In this one, I was hobbling on a crooked, narrow path. A cold wind seeped into my body. I looked down. My leg was gone. Where the joint would have been attached was a gaping hole, an entrance for the wind. I tried to scream but couldn't. A female form hovered in the distance. Her features were a blur. The sky was white. I was paralyzed with fear and yet I moved inexorably toward her. And then, out of nowhere, a curtain. Brown, filthy, almost transparent. The woman was behind it and calling to me. My good leg was leaden, the other an open wound. Blood trickled, streamed, and then gushed out. Still I couldn't stop. I reached the curtain. I was trembling, convulsing, but steadied myself. I slid open the flimsy material, staining it red. Feet, torso, breasts, neck. No face. The woman had no face.

I propped myself on a pillow, flicked on the light and grabbed my bag from the nightstand. I took out a stick and my camera. It was dark by the time I'd arrived last night. Traffic was slow due to the rain. I'd been tired but had gone to the bar, the Havana Room, because it was famous for its live music. In fact, the Inn itself had become a tourist destination of sorts. All I recall of the décor is that it was dark and moody, but I could have just been projecting myself onto it. Bunky Valdez, a rotund, jovial saxophonist, and his orchestra were playing. I had a couple of drinks. Maybe more than a couple. And dancing. Yes, I danced, slow, the only way I really could, with a few of the locals. One, I remember, reminded me of Penny. This dame didn't wear a bonnet, though. Her hair was blonde, sleek and long. But she wore very little make-up, and her face had Penny's same pointed shape. She even smelled a little like her. I held her close, closer than I should have. And I had a steak.

My tongue was thick. I needed coffee. I untangled myself from the sheets and scooted to the edge of the bed. My leg felt airy, but when I put pressure on it I didn't fall. The curtain covering the window was brown and white striped, a distorted combination of which I'd obviously incorporated into my dream. I paused and drew it open. No demons. No rain. The sun streamed in and glistened off the Bakersfield sign. The giant blue letters, spelling out the city's name, spanned the entire width of the street. A symbol of substance, a mark of belonging. I snapped a picture of it.

~

I was now hungry, too, but I sat by the window for a while longer reading the motel pamphlet. It stated that Bakersfield was named for Thomas Baker, an Ohio lawyer who settled there during the gold rush. Plain and simple. But, according to the encyclopedia I'd consulted at home, that was only partially true. The original settlement, washed away by a flood, was founded by a German. So what's in a name, anyway? It can reveal but it can also deceive. Or simply be inadequate. Take my childhood illness. Over-stimulated, anxious, depressed, they didn't really know what name to give it. I fell somewhere in-between. Episodes, the doctors called them. When they were bad, a hospital stay was prescribed to snap me out of it. Give me some drugs, talk a little and send me home. It usually worked, but no one knew what I really had.

Or even Cotard's, the name of my current disorder. It explains some, but leaves much out. The doctor said my case was mild, but I've come to think of it as more of a variation on a theme, an as-of-yet unlabeled condition waiting for science to catch up. Either way, the name didn't help me on VJ Day. Truman proclaimed it a holiday, a time to rejoice in defeat of the enemy. But that day I experienced an insurrection. My leg had never felt more foreign, never less a part of me than when families reunited, when soldiers were heading home.

I tried to ignore it, join in the fun. But the urge was too powerful. This enemy needed to be defeated, too, so I tried to kill it. I didn't think I was dead, like some of those other poor souls with Cotard's, but I wanted my leg to be.

The idea came to me at the downtown L.A. parade. I'd limped along Broadway, watching the revelers, trying in vain to catch a bit of the gaiety. Confetti fell, lovers embraced, city officials waved from their floats. "Happy Days Are Here Again!" rang out across the basin.

Scattered in the crowd were also the wounded. Grateful to be alive, I'd imagined, lucky to be breathing, but knowing they would never be the same. I wandered the streets, drawn to these men. The ones with bandages and slings, and particularly the amputees.

One without an arm. Another with hooks for hands. I searched their faces for the inner conflict. But what I saw instead was a kind of bliss. They toasted. They sang. They danced to their own melody. Even a soldier missing his leg. Couldn't have been more than twenty-three. A red-headed beanpole, swimming in his starched, colorfully medaled uniform. On crutches, his curled up pant leg hid his stump. But his smile was broad, without any seeming constraint. He swung a girl in his arms, easily, as if the absence of his leg had given him extra strength. His sense of balance seemed superhuman. I gazed at him, feeling my good limb move to his rhythm.

It was a leap in logic, a sign of insanity, if I weren't aware that it was. But I suddenly knew what to do. I'd been depressed. More than usual. A client had committed suicide the week before, just a month after I'd won his case. A worker had fallen at his shoe factory, leaving the man paralyzed on one side. It was a freak accident, one that should have resulted in nothing more than a sprain. His lawyer blamed a wet floor but the jury didn't buy it. My client was relieved and paid me handsomely. But a few days later, his wife died unexpectedly. He shot himself after the funeral, leaving me a note thanking me again for my efforts.

I'd never been so clear-eyed, so certain of how to restore my sense of wellbeing. If one has a boil, lance it. A deformity, repair it. A cancer, excise it. I would rid myself of the leg, like the moldy piece of an otherwise fresh cake. Then I would feel whole.

The timing was perfect. I had just started a two-month sabbatical, so I'd have time to recover. My leg had all but disappeared anyway—I would just finish the job. Not like some maniac, not like a tormented Van Gogh. There was no fit of rage. No twisted motive. I just wanted to be myself.

The idea revealed itself to me one step at a time. First, booze. A lot of it. Next, a sock, one of my knee-highs, and some of that twine I used for packages. Third, tie off the leg and prop it up on the wall to prevent blood from flowing into it. Fourth, wait. Wait for the numbness, the red and purple to set in. Wait some more. Then, call the ambulance, say I thought I'd be bitten by a black widow, tried to seal off the poison and had fainted. By that time, the doctors would have no choice but to amputate the ischemic flesh.

Not surprisingly, the drinking part was easy, although halfway through I did consider the effect this change might have on my job. Even though I already felt handicapped by my aliment, it might be harder to find clients. People are put off by deformities. Then again, I might earn more sympathy in court. Juries tend to favor the less fortunate. And what about women? There, too, it might be an advantage. With the agony gone, with my body really mine, who knew what pleasure I might be capable of giving?

I tied the sock, tight, and lay down. I fell asleep, maybe for an hour. When I awoke, the leg was hot. I shut my eyes again, for how long I didn't know. Then, pain! I shifted my gaze to the floor. My shoes must have brought in that dirt, I thought, noticing a faint outline of my footprints. I pulled the sock tighter, moaned. I wanted the numbness to spread, to anesthetize me. But it didn't. I was sweating, nauseated. My apartment was stifling. I envisioned a pool, or no, the ocean. Not blue. Grey and turbulent. And then, in the distance, a ship. An old rickety ship rocking on the waves. The Pequod. And Ahab. And his peg. His damned pegged leg. Thump, thump, thump. Was it is left, or right? Echoing on the clapboards. Thump, thump, thump!

No. No more! I ripped the twine, tore off the sock and called for an ambulance. The emergency room doctor asked me questions that I barely remember. All I know is that I was released under my own recognizance with a bandaged limb that still wasn't mine.

The Inn had a hint of the Mediterranean, with ceramic tiles and a pleasantly trickling fountain. The lobby was decorated for Christmas. A flocked tree sparkled with tinsel, and a wreath hung over the counter.

"Look at that, Mommy!"

A boy, around five, was pointing to a life-sized crèche that stood in the corner of the room. How could I have missed it? It was a standard scene, but enormous, something you'd see in front of a church.

"That's the baby Jesus," the mother said. "You can look, but don't touch."

The child did exactly the opposite, grabbing the donkey as well as the baby, nearly toppling over the manger. The mother glanced around apologetically and marched him away. But the boy looked back, seemingly at me. As if to say, "remember?" And I was remembering something. Another Christmas. In front of another manger. My own mother. Her hand, soft, in mine.

"Quite a piece," the desk clerk said.

"Excuse me?"

"The nativity scene. Hand-carved by some nuns. You should take a closer look. The workmanship is superb."

I did.

"Amazing, huh?" the clerk yelled out while I examined it. I nodded, but was more disturbed than amazed. The carving was indeed well executed, but the figures were grimacing, as if none of them could stand each other's company, more macabre than holy.

There was a bright restaurant near the lobby, and I was hungry, but couldn't stomach their Christmas soundtrack. I opted for the empty patio. The air was a little chilly, but post-rain fresh.

I bought a copy of the *Bakersfield Californian* and ordered eggs Benedict from a waiter who resembled me, in a fun house mirror sort of way. Brown, but long where I was wide, fat where I was thin. A Gregory Peck caricature. The eggs were delicious, creamy and rich, worth the change from my usual fried. I scanned the headlines.

STORM SOAKS KERN WITH NEEDED RAIN; PLANNERS TO STUDY MOVE TO WIDEN JAIL PROPERTY; MERCHANTS WARNED OF YULE ACTIVITY OF CHECK ARTISTS.

The usual. Weather and crime. But there was comfort in reading it. Concrete and limited in scope, counterbalancing the dark, ambiguous nature of my psyche.

I chewed on a cinnamon stick and hovered over the movie section. "Trail of the Yukon," "The Secret Garden," and "Saboteur," a new Hitchcock spy thriller of all things, were playing. Saboteur. I couldn't hear the word without thinking of my father. Without seeing him in handcuffs, without tasting salt on my tongue.

I asked for the check as I glanced at the "Today in Washington" section. The waiter wrote it up, eyeing the paper over my shoulder.

PRESIDENT, SECRETARY STUDY POLICY. President Truman has held a lengthy and important telephone conference with Secretary of State Acheson on national security. An air of mystery surrounded the conference with his No. 1 Cabinet Chief. Its nature remained officially secret.

He nodded and handed me the bill.

# 11

# CRITICAL TERRAIN

I pressed on the gas, whooshing by fields glossy from rain. The sky was clear, with the exception of a few restive clouds. My window was partially open, and the cool air brought with it a sharp onion scent, although the nearby crops appeared to be grapes. I turned on the radio, twisted the knob past a breathy evangelist and a jingle for Crispy Potato Chips. For a moment, I listened to a sportscaster discussing the playoffs. The Rams were playing the Eagles on December 18th at the L.A. Coliseum. "The Rams will lose," he proclaimed, as if there were no other possibility. He was probably right.

*America. They don't have real football, Mijo. Mexico has real football.*

Go fuck yourself, Pop. I love the sport. The L.A. Bulldogs and now the Rams.

I stopped on a classical station just as traffic slowed. The reception was weak, but adequate. The announcer was about to play Brahms' Piano Concerto No. 2 in B-flat. "Like a fabulous journey," he said. "Breathtaking beauty in the first movement, dark and violent passion in the second, sublime cello solo in the third, spirited with a tinge of the gypsy in the last. A range of moods and emotions."

I crawled along with the other cars and listened as the signal grew stronger. The broadcaster was right. The Brahms was spectacular, a moving accompaniment to the tranquil scenery.

A Bach cantata was next, followed by a Schumann lullaby. I yawned, having gone only about five miles. It was two o'clock. Must be an accident, I thought. My stomach was growling. While I kept a lookout for a café, I noticed the start of a new crop. Trees, young and willowy, with narrow trunks and light green leaves. They were positioned diagonally at meticulously spaced intervals. ENTERING WALNUT COUNTRY, a billboard read.

I should have guessed, recalling something about Central Valley soil producing the best walnuts in the country. Probably from my grandmother, who incorporated the nut into her diet. She'd combine them with raisins and keep a cache in her apron pocket, munching as she did her chores. The raisins made her sweet, she said, and the nuts gave her strength, a claim she'd prove by cracking the shells with a spoon. I often stole a handful, much to her delight, even though she'd pretend to shoo me away. I loved that game. Especially because she couldn't keep a straight face, because she couldn't lie. Or so I thought.

I kept my eyes peeled but still no café. My gut felt hollow. I should have brought a snack, but I hadn't, and now I was starting to feel the kind of irritation that only food could cure.

Another five miles. Same sluggish pace. Same fertile trees, but with nothing edible for purchase.

I was just about to cannibalize one of my sticks when I spotted the workers, their vibrant shirts billowing in the breeze. Red, yellow, blue, contrasting with the monochromatic symmetry of the land. There, and there, and there. Shirts with rolled-up sleeves on the brown-skinned men. Brown and hard, like the crop they were tending.

Hoeing, picking. Some hunched over. A few on ladders. Most wearing hats. Workers. Laborers.

*Your people, Mijo. Never forget. Your people.*

I pulled over, turned off the ignition and followed them with my eyes. Watched the colors bend and reach. My own shirt was white, loose with an open collar. But just then it squeezed my chest, as if it were suddenly the wrong size, so I unbuttoned it all the way.

The sun beat down through the front window, shining on a Rorschach of splattered insects. I reached for my flask. Not wise on an empty stomach but good for everything else. The rum hit me fast, starting to quiet my leg even before its initial scorch receded. My head spun, too, making me briefly queasy, but soon righted itself, smoothing out into a familiar hum. I continued to watch the workers, but through a softer filter, like the one I had recently purchased for my camera. Here was a living tableau. More Renoir than Jacob Riis.

Maybe it was the whiff of dust it kicked up, maybe the ripple effect of its lumbering tires. Whichever, I sensed the pick-up truck before I saw it. An old, black pick-up, clumsily navigating the dirt road that led into the field. I knew that truck. Knew the road, too. Or one just like it.

~

*"Hurry up, Mijo."*

*"Coming!"*

*It's my birthday. I'm thirteen and Pop is taking me on a surprise trip. I usually don't like surprises. I like to know and plan. But I'm excited about this. Pop says I'm finally old enough.*

*"We're off to the fields," Pop tells my grandmother.*

*She gives him that worried look. She's always worried,*

especially about me. But Pop just smiles and kisses her forehead.

We stop by one of his grocery stores. He owns three now. He tells the manager he'll be back tomorrow. Then we head east in the Model T that Pop says one day will be mine. On the way, he talks about Rochester Farms. He buys his produce from them, and they've hired him because the pickers like to talk to him. He's called a liaison. Mr. Rochester likes to keep his pickers happy.

I ask him what they talk to him about, and he says that for now he is just listening to their complaints.

As we drive, he pats my leg. "Thirteen," he says. "Handsome like your Pop. Women will love you."

We arrive a couple of hours later at the fields. A pick-up truck is waiting. We sit in the open back. The truck rattles side-to-side, as if at any moment it could topple over. Pop offers me a section of orange. The juice spills on my pants, makes my hands sticky. We pass the pickers. They all wave to Pop. Some drop their tools and follow us on foot.

The truck stops at an old shack. We hop off and go in. There's a table and chairs. Soon the pickers arrive. They all shake hands. Pop introduces me. "My brilliant son," he says. He asks me to sit with them as they talk about the conditions. The low wages, long hours, filthy cabins. Then Pop sends me outside for a while, like he does when we visit his girlfriends.

I walk through the fields. The air is pungent and sweet.

After a while we leave, but the surprise isn't over. The truck drives us farther inland, to an area overrun with dried out bushes. Around a bend is another shack.

"This is what I really wanted you to see, Mijo. My hideout."
"Hideout?"
"Yeah, like Capone! It's where I go when I want to be alone."

I'm surprised. I have a hideout, too. It's where I go when I feel scared, when the world is too loud, when I miss my Pop. Down by the L.A. River. Just a concrete tunnel. But it's cool and quiet.

He leads me inside. I recognize a few things. A blanket, a picture. So there's that chair! We sit on the floor. He tells me to wait, gets up and comes back with a bottle.

"Thirteen," he says again.

A magic number, I think.

"Time for your initiation." He opens the bottle. Tequila. I've had some before but I don't want to spoil it for him.

"Salud!"

"Salud!," I say, coughing a little, on purpose.

# 12

## A.W.O.L.

The pick-up truck had stopped, and with it the toil. The workers were climbing off ladders, gathering. I craned my neck out the window. They were taking a break, maybe lunch. But it was late, almost three o'clock, the sun already starting to give in. I yawned. I, too, was starting to give in.

~

I locked away the gun, grabbed my bag and got out of the car. It was easy to slip into the field unnoticed. Too easy. No wire, no fence, just the sign. Soon, I was surrounded by trees. Green and yellowish husks the size of golf balls hung from the branches. The ground was still wet, my shoes clumping with mud. My leg seemed to be holding up, but the rest of me felt at odds with reality, as if I were outside myself. Watching a movie, or a play, where I was the star with the props off-center.

"Hey there!"

The voice was behind me. I turned.

"¿Qué pasa? Can I help you?"

The man's arms were folded, his legs spread. He was tall. No hat. Wavy black hair. His shirt was red. Or was it yellow? I couldn't make it out. Blue? The colors blurred. The sun shone bright, as if reversing its course, as if it were high noon. My head spun again, worse than before. "I'd like...I'd like to...*Me gustaría...*"

~

"*Se está despertando...*"

I felt my eyes flutter open. The man who spoke was standing over me, hazy at first but gradually defined. He was holding a lantern, watching me with a look that fluctuated between concern and contempt.

"Better?" he said. He crouched and leaned in so close I could hear him breathe. His features were broader than they'd appeared from afar and almost perfectly symmetrical, as if they'd been measured with a ruler.

"Yes," I said, although I wasn't really sure. All I knew was that I was awake, supine on a hard cot. Or was I?

"*¿Hablas español, verdad?*"

"Not really."

"You passed out."

"I'm sorry," I said, wondering if this was a new symptom. I sat up and scanned the room, a one-window, concrete box with a linoleum floor, a couple of other cots, and scattered chairs. A pickers' cabin, I presumed, newer but just as basic as those I'd visited in my youth. Two other men stood nearby, their long shadows guarding the door.

"You don't have to be sorry for *that.*" He pinched my arm, raising my skin into a fleshy peak. "You need water," he said, rolling his Rs, his thick Spanish accent just then fully registering.

Dehydrated. That's all it was. "I haven't eaten either," I said. "I was looking for a truck stop."

"Nothing like that for miles." He coughed, looked at me hard.

"I searched through your pocket," he said. "Found your wallet. Driver's license says you're Andrew Martin."

I swallowed, or at least tried to. Andrew Martin. 702 Crescent. Los Angeles. Height: 6'2". Weight: 185 lbs. Eyes: Brown. He must have rummaged through my receipts, notes, maybe even stroked Emerson's feather. I felt violated. Plus, there was cash in my wallet, a lot of it. "That's right."

"I'm the supervisor," he said. "Name's Oscar. We found your camera. Booze and pills, too, in your bag there," pointing to somewhere I couldn't see.

"Just to keep me company," I said flatly.

"Not for me to judge."

"*No se parece a un* Andrew Martin," one of the others said.

"He said you don't look like an Andrew Martin," Oscar said.

"So I've been told. But I'm American. Changed my name."

"Not for me to judge either," Oscar said, staring at me coolly. "I just want to know what the hell you're doing here. We're busy people, if you haven't noticed."

"I feel foolish," I said. "Clearly, I made a mistake, and I apologize for putting you out. If you can forget about it, I'll go as I came."

"Not yet," Oscar said.

Maybe it was his chin, which he held at an upward pose. Or his commanding tone. Whichever, his declaration seemed to hold the force of law.

"We need to be sure," he said. "We should have called the boss, but we thought maybe you were spying on us for him."

"Spying?" I almost laughed. "No."

"We saw your business card. You're a lawyer. Could have been eavesdropping, seeing if we're organizing, planning to take pictures with that camera."

"I wasn't," I said. "I'm not."

"Maybe you're working for the government. Looking for illegals. If that's it, you're out of luck. We're all *braceros*. Contracted."

"No. I lost my way is all." I started to stand. "Please," I said. "It's late. I'm already behind schedule and don't know the roads."

He pushed me down. "Precisely why you shouldn't drive. Not in your condition. And not until we're convinced."

Oscar summoned the others to the corner of the room. They spoke in low voices, but I could hear the questioning pitch, the curiosity. And here and there a word: *la pasma*, *el dandy*, *loco*. They huddled for what seemed like hours. Deciding my fate. Fading in and out of view. I tried to get up again, but fell back. I couldn't move, heard myself call out. "Help! *¡Ayúdame!*"

Oscar turned. "What's wrong?"

"I can't...." but I could, suddenly I *could* move."

"Can't what?"

"I... Please, just let me go."

He shook his head, looked at the others. "Blanca's waiting. Let's take him with us. Maybe food will jog his memory."

Oscar and another man then raised me up. Someone else grabbed my bag, and, I hoped my wallet. "We're heading to my place," Oscar said, "over there about fifty yards."

It was nearly dark. Nothing was right, and yet the night air revived me, the loam and nutty blossoms acting like smelling salts. Things came into focus. Purple, a sliver of moon, muffled voices from the other cabins. There were eight identical units, clustered together on a plot of barren dirt. Oscar led the way with his lantern, revealing a clothesline, a bicycle, an outhouse.

The aroma wafting out from Oscar's cabin turned my attention. I knew it instantly, even though I hadn't encountered this particular variant since I was a kid visiting my aunt in Oaxaca during Christmas. Banana and bay leaf. Chile burned to a crisp. I could smell it all. Even the secret ingredient. A sprig of history? A pinch of time? I didn't know what it was, and yet I recognized it. Blood maybe.

"Mole," I said. My aunt's specialty. Smoky and primordial, although I didn't have those words to describe it back then. The flavor echoed the aroma, but was secondary to it. My aunt had echoed something, too, but I couldn't place that either. She was my father's sister, but she didn't look like him. Her hair was jet black, but her skin was a few shades lighter, and she was petite, with a heart-shaped face and hazel eyes.

Inside, a plump woman with her back to us stood at a small stove. She turned and smiled, until she saw me.

"One more for dinner, *chica*," Oscar said.

She sighed, as if this were a common occurrence. Oscar went over to her, wrapped his arms around her round waist. "A wanderer," he said. "*Americano*."

She cocked her head at me. "*¿No hablas español?*"

"Not much."

"Is okay. Little English. You can stay."

"Blanca thinks I'm too generous," Oscar said. "I sometimes invite a worker or two over from another field. We're more privileged than most around here, mainly because my *abuela* took care of the owner's father as a child. He made me the supervisor and gave me a few extras. Although the best extra is my wife's cooking," he said, in an abruptly kinder mood. "Touched by the gods."

I inhaled. "I believe it," I said. But I didn't quite believe the scene I was in. Some gringo's idea of Mexicans. The domestic, the laborer, accepting of their roles, unquestioning of their meager lot in life.

Blanca turned again, still stirring. "*¿Quién es usted?*"

Oscar smirked at me, with a knowingness that made me squirm. One minute he seemed friendly, the next hostile. Keeping me off balance.

"Andrew," I said.

"Andrew Martin," Oscar said to his wife. "From Los Angeles. A lawyer."

She glanced from Oscar to me and back again. "Dinner is almost ready," she said. "Wash your hands."

Oscar filled a bowl with water and handed me some soap. I sat down on the seat Blanca offered. "*Gracias,*" I said.

Blanca met my eyes. She had a penetrating gaze.

The cabin was slightly bigger than the other, and there were no cots, just a double bed. There was also a table and chairs, a large tattered rug and a rudimentary icebox. A guitar leaned against a wall, on which also hung a black and white photograph of a baby. And then, the odd things. A cloud in the shape of a birdcage, dangling from the ceiling. The floor: dirt to the eye, marble to the touch.

Oscar lit two candles whose previously melted wax had created drape-like patterns on the ceramic holders.

"You said you're *braceros?*" I said.

Oscar raised one brow and kept it there. "Yeah, why?"

"I just...I don't know." But I did know. Despite my usual tendencies, I had some sympathy for them. Especially because as seasonal laborers, *braceros* had to regularly leave their homes, performing back-breaking work for pennies.

"We're trying to become citizens, but I'm sure you know how that goes."

"You mean because I'm Chicano or a lawyer?" I said.

"Both. Come to think of it, it would be pretty clever of the government to hire someone who resembled us."

"That should prove I'm telling the truth. The government is many things, but clever isn't one of them."

"You may be right there. Our daughter," he said, noticing me eye the photograph. "She died two years ago."

"I'm sorry."

I moved closer to the photo. The baby was propped up on a pillow. A bow was pinned onto her sparse, wispy hair. She was chubby and smiling.

"Married? Children?" he said.

"No." I glanced at Blanca and imagined her suffering. Probably would have sold her soul to have her baby back. Unlike those unwed mothers, I thought, desperate to give theirs away. Unlike my own mother.

The table was set for five. Blanca added a setting and placed a vase with some little yellow flowers on the table. A common gesture, but one that struck me as courageous, even noble. It was a choice she had made. To rise above her circumstances, her tragedy, to bring beauty into the darkness.

Oscar leaned over the arrangement and sniffed. "Bird foot lotus," he said. "Grows wild around here."

Bird foot? I knew only one bird foot. Four digits, wrinkled flesh, spindly claws clamped over his hand-carved wooden perch. Was Emerson still in Martha's favor? I wanted to stroke his head, hear him call my name. "Lovely," I said.

The mole was rich but not heavy, smoky but not ashy, chocolaty but not sweet. The same taste as my aunt's, but somehow unique.

I devoured it, asked for a second helping and then a third. My capacity seemed endless. I asked for a fourth, a mistake I thought for a moment. My stomach rippled, intestines cramped. But the feeling soon passed, and I sopped up the remaining sauce with a warm tortilla.

I could feel everyone watching me. "I guess I was even hungrier than I thought."

"There's more where that came from," Oscar said.

I couldn't imagine ever wanting to eat again, but I took that as a sign that maybe he had softened toward me. I was encouraged even further when Blanca cleared the dishes and brought out a full bottle of mezcal.

"Another extra," Oscar said. "For special occasions."

"I'm honored," I said, feeling as if the cameras were rolling again.

"Don't be. Tonight is our wedding anniversary," he said, kissing his wife's hand.

"Congratulations."

"We don't have the time or money to celebrate as we'd like, but this helps," he said, twisting the lid. "You lucked out, showing up today, Mr. *Martin*. I still don't trust you, but yesterday I think I would have just called the cops."

I supposed I should have felt grateful, but the bottle caught my attention. I recognized the label. It had been my father's brand, so divine, he'd claimed, that it gave credence to the myth that mezcal was discovered after lightning struck an agave plant, releasing its precious juices from the core.

One of the other men, Miguel, rolled some cigarettes and offered me one. I shook my head, started to search my bag, now in my possession, for a stick. But I reconsidered. Watched myself reconsider, that is. Listened to a voice offstage saying it would be like declining a peace pipe. Only this once, it said, even though I nearly cried with joy at the taste of my old lover.

"What kind of lawyer are you?" Oscar said.

"Defense." I took a sip of the mezcal. It burned, the heat fanning out to every part of me.

"What kind of defense?"

"General," I said, feeling the heat begin to melt my joints. I held out my glass.

"You think you should?" Oscar said.

"Probably not."

He smiled a little and poured. "What kind of general?"

I could have lied, but I decided he might trust me more if I simply told the truth. "I defend the rich and powerful."

"You mean like my boss?"

So he hadn't given up. "*Like* him, perhaps," I said, "but not him."

Smoke swirled in the makeshift home, having little route for escape. Like fog, it settled in pockets, one of which reflected in Oscar's glassy, almost tender-looking eyes. The booze had started to cut through the surface, releasing us both from initial impressions. Oscar's shoulders dropped, his back rounded. Then he reached for his guitar and started strumming.

For a while, the notes were random, and I exhaled. This very strange evening would soon end, and I would be back on the road, left with my own thoughts.

But first, what was that? The beginning of order. A scale? No, a melody. Hardly recognizable. The key was off, the tempo slower. I prided myself on my ability to identify a song, often from a single measure. I listened harder, picking up a thread, but not the finished garment, until Oscar started to sing...

*"Yo no soy americano*
*Pero comprendo el inglés.*
*Yo lo aprendí con mi hermano*
*al derecho y al revés*
*A cualquier americano*
*Lo hago temblar a mis pies."*

I moaned under my breath, already hearing the next verse and the next. Coincidental. Too coincidental.

It was a *corrido*, the musical equivalent of a piñata. Colorful, simple, with a sugary reward. Not a lollipop, but candy-coated Mexican history. At least that's the way I thought of it. Particularly this one, about Joaquín Murrieta, gold-miner turned bandit and murderer. How could I forget? It was my father's theme song, the one he would whistle, hum, use to put me to sleep. Like my father, Oscar would no doubt say Murrieta's crimes were justified, that the gringos who supposedly raped his wife deserved it. Fine. But his actions, idealized and mythologized, meant to inspire young Mexicans everywhere, were still against the law.

> *"Cuando apenas era un nino*
> *huérfano a mi me dejaron*
> *Nadie me hizo ni un cariño..."*

"When I was barely a child, I was left an orphan. No one gave me a bit of affection..."

Oh Christ did I remember those lines. Excuses. Justifications for unsavory behavior. Heard them a million times in court. Poor girl, the lawyer pleads to the jury. Have pity. Her stepmother hated her. That's why she stole from her landlady. Or look at that unlucky man. Scarred in his youth. Bullied by his peers. That's why he took a knife to his better-looking brother. Mitigating circumstances. Be lenient, your Honor.

The mezcal kept coming, and I kept drinking. So did Oscar, whose gentle baritone turned raspy. Soon, he started to slur his words, so much so that they lost their meaning and thus, for me, their sting. Everyone was deep under the influence by then, swaying, chiming in, attempting to harmonize with this drunken bard.

Blanca was the first to laugh at the painful cacophony. A giggle really. Light and sweet. But it caught on like wildfire. I laughed, loud and long, until tears streamed down my cheeks. And in the quiet space following, when we were all catching our breath, I thought: *¿Por qué no?* Why not tell them? Then Oscar would believe me. *¿Por qué no?*

"Carlos Martínez," I blurted out. "Carlos. Andrés. Martínez."

Oscar hushed his guitar. Carlos Martínez. The name reverberated off the plaster, ricocheted from corner to corner. It could have lit the candles if they weren't already aflame. They all looked at me as if I'd taken the Lord's name in vain.

"What of him?" Oscar said.

"You've heard of him, of course."

"Of course."

"He was my father," I said.

Silence.

"I'm his son," I said, approaching the reality from the other end.

Oscar turned to Blanca and then the others. Yes, the resemblance was there, they were thinking. Striking, now that they realized it. My father had been front-page news, was a minor legend in their world.

For a while they just sat there, communicating by smoke rings. Then Oscar resumed his strumming, changing the tune, shifting to a minor key: "Carlos Martínez, led an uprising, helped the workers. In the cover of night, he led an uprising, helped the workers..."

"Yeah, he led an uprising all right," I said. "But you know what I say to that? Fuck that. Fuck him."

"What's matter with you?" Blanca said.

Oscar touched my shoulder. "*¿Qué pasa?*"

I glanced at his hand, powerful and dark, and gently shook

it off. "Can I have another smoke?" I said to Miguel, who was still sitting motionless.

Oscar lit my cigarette. I dragged on it effortlessly, as if we'd never broken up. I blew a few smoke rings of my own and then, oddly, became very calm. "My father isn't who you think he was."

He put down the guitar and poured another round. I drank mine down, sat back and attempted to cross my legs.

"Who do I think he was?" Oscar said.

Pioneer. Organizer. Mexican workers' rights movement. Led an uprising, the one in the song. Worked for Rochester Farms. Pretended to help quell worker unrest while actually encouraging rebellion. Like a pied piper, got all those pickers to pour salt into the irrigation ditches. Believed the mischief would hasten compliance, would result in higher wages, better working conditions.

Oscar nodded even though I hadn't said a word. He was reading my mind. His lips didn't move either, but I knew he could hear me so I continued:

But Rochester employees showed up. A fight broke out. Someone was killed. Carlos was arrested. Murdered in prison. By a guard, claiming self-defense. Found innocent.

"We all knew otherwise," Oscar finally said, responding to my thoughts, vocalizing the only point of contention.

He started to explain. Slurring again and in Spanish. Indeed, we were talking in Spanish now, communication shifting from the mind to the tongue. In Spanish! How? Thought I'd willed it away. Was it the booze? The mole?

"But," he said in an exaggerated manner, pointing his finger for emphasis, "the most important thing is that after Carlos', I mean, your father's, death, Rochester *did* increase wages. The tactics—intended to be non-violent—are models for us all. *Salud!*"

Blanca got up and opened the window, letting in air that had turned bitterly cold. "What about your mother?" she said.

"Pardon?"

"Your mother."

What the hell was this? I looked around, half-expecting to see Penny float in on her cape.

"You haven't mentioned her."

I hadn't mentioned a lot of things. "She died when I was five."

"That's hard."

I waited for her to sit back down before I answered.

"I did have problems as a boy. My father *said* he loved me."

"And he didn't?" Blanca said, as if that were an impossibility.

"I don't know. He accepted me, tried to comfort me, held me to a high standard. Now and then, he showered me with attention. But you can't make up for all the absences in a day. Most of the time, he was gone."

"Is that what brought you?" Oscar said. "To find out if he's here?" He chuckled.

I would have bashed him in the face if I didn't know he was drunk.

"Come on," he said. "That's just a child's view. We all want more from our fathers."

"Maybe. But it wasn't just that," I said.

"What then?"

I stood and walked around the room. Was I limping? I couldn't tell. I sat back down, asked for another cigarette. And I continued to drink.

"I was twenty-one the night of the uprising. I wasn't there. But my friend was. My only true friend, old man Rochester's son."

Someone shuddered. Miguel, I think. But they all sat up, shifting in their seats. And me? It had been so long since I let myself think of James that I almost felt as if I were inventing him. Tall and lanky, wildish auburn hair. Intelligent, a thinker, with a heavy stutter. That stutter is what I remembered most, the first time I'd ever heard one so pronounced.

"We met when we were both fourteen, at a party at his house. You know, my father was a grocer. Made his living supplying Mexican delicacies to rich *Angelenos*. I helped carry some things in for my father that night. James was sitting outside, reading. He looked up and smiled."

I was talking to Oscar but visualizing James, remembering how I'd glared back at him, as if to say, don't condescend to me, gringo. *Spoiled* gringo, my father would have added.

~

*"Wha, wha...what's your problem?" James says, following me into the house.*

*I ignore him. But he keeps on. "Hey. I'm James. Wh...what's your name?"*

*I put down the groceries and turn, ready to shove him for what I think is a joke. But he smiles again and blushes. "I stutter. Maybe you didn't understand me."*

*In that moment, I know the impediment, and his reaction, are real. I also realize that he knows something about pain. About having to fight for acceptance, about not feeling at one with the world. It was all there in that blush.*

*I feel the chip on my shoulder droop a little. "Andrés," I say. My name is Andrés."*

*James smiles more broadly. "I st...st...utter to humiliate my father," he says with a chuckle. "I'm not the s...s...son he dreamed of."*

*That comment takes me aback, but it also draws me to James.*

*"Come on," he says, "let me show you the house."*

*Mansion is more like it. High, vaulted ceilings, marble floors, modern furniture, art filling every available space. A Negro maid in the kitchen.*

"Some place," I say.

"I'd rather live in a d...dugout."

I laugh at that, but when we reach his bedroom I realize that he's serious. Baseball is clearly his passion. Bats and gloves, balls and ticket stubs occupy a good deal of the room, a giant field of a space in which my entire house could almost fit. I browse his collection, which includes a signed glossy photo of Babe Ruth. But I'm more intrigued with his floor-to-ceiling bookshelf. Crammed with all kinds of titles. 'The Strange Case of Doctor Jekyll and Mr. Hyde,' 'Great Expectations,' 'White Fang.' 'A History of Pancho Villa,' which I'm surprised to see. Several Hardy Boys mysteries. Books on hurricanes and tornados. One shelf devoted to National Geographic. He, like me, must read to learn as well as escape, I think. And then there are the girly magazines, hidden in a drawer the maid never bothers to clean. Quite a collection. Some even I, who thought I'd seen them all, didn't know about. After some careful analysis of those, our friendship is sealed.

~

"Despite our vast differences," I said to Oscar, who'd come back into view, "our fathers tolerated the friendship, relieved that we had at least connected with someone our own age. We'd scared other boys off with our oddities. We were sensitive, brooding, too inward to be one of the gang. Girls liked us, but they felt sorry for us, too, which made us push them away. And James also had lost his mother, something we intuited in the spark missing in each other's eyes. We were like Pythias and Damon, without the happy ending. He was the only person outside of my family that I confided in about my problems. He was the only one, period, that truly understood them."

Oscar cleared his throat as if to interject. He'd heard everything, one way or another. But I knew that if I stopped, I might lose my voice for good.

"James was there when the fighting broke out, with a daughter of one of the workers. They'd been secretly seeing each other for months. My father said it was an accident. That James appeared out of nowhere, that the gun was only intended to startle. Unintentional. Unexpected. But he died on the scene. Bullet hit in just the wrong place."

The mezcal bottle was empty. Exhaustion seemed to have added another layer of haze to the air. Blanca's hair had come undone, Miguel was slumped in his chair. Oscar's head was nearly in his lap.

"Yeah, he said it was an accident. But it wasn't. The girl's father murdered James. And my own father, the mighty Carlos Martínez, the hero of your *corrido*, egged him on."

~

Steering wheel, window, radio. Body, cramped. Head, throbbing.

Where was I? I looked out. There were the fields. The shirts. The pickers. A tractor. But the sky. The sky was grey and orange. The sun had dropped. But it wasn't dark. I sat up. Christ. I was in my car. I shook myself. A dream?

I opened the car door, got out. Breathed in, trying to get a whiff of the mole. Oscar, Blanca. The lot of them. Reading my mind. Hearing my thoughts. No wonder. All a dream. Another goddamn dream.

~

It was dusk, traffic was light, and I was speeding, eager to make up time. I was almost a day behind now. The dream was a dream.

A dream. But as the shadow spread, completely shading one side of the hill, I wondered if I was doomed to that darkening side, permanently excluded from the sunlight that gleamed on the other. James. Rochester. My father. A triad of love and grief. But all I could do about them was dream.

I opened the window. Reality. That's what I needed. And a few seconds later, I got it. A bird, real, wings bloodied, dead in the road. Limp and battered, with no one to grieve for it. I swerved and pulled over, grabbed my cane and waited for a few cars to pass. Then I hobbled out into the road and nudged the carrion into the dirt. I carved a little hole with the cane, pushed the bird in, and uttered something like a prayer. I returned to the car and sat for a moment, pleased at my action. The gods appeared to be in a listening mood, so I made another request. A phone. What I needed was a phone and a gallon of black coffee.

# 14

## RETREAT

"One dollar and fifty cents, please," the operator said.

I dropped the coins into the slots and waited. The phone booth in Fresno's Hotel Californian, like the rest of the no doubt once elegant Beaux Arts structure, had seen better days. The wood was chipped and sticky. Carved into it were names, hearts and obscenities. I sipped the coffee, which was also well past its prime.

"Hello, hello?" Martha sounded hurried, as if she were en route to her nest.

"Martha, this is Andrew Martin."

"Emerson's fine, dear."

I felt myself blush. "You know me too well."

Birds called in the background. I listened in vain for Emerson's plaintive tone.

"He's actually found a lady friend," she said.

"Oh?"

"Yes, a tiny yellow finch. But don't worry, I'm keeping an eye on them."

"Good. I wouldn't want him to get her into any trouble."

She warbled out a laugh.

"Where is he now?"

"Resting. Leg up, you know."

Yes, I knew.

"Now, you do your job, Mr. Martin, and don't worry about your boy. I've got to run... Oh. Oh, wait, I forgot. A woman called the other day. Asking if I knew how to reach you."

"A woman?"

"Yes, um, S. Started with an S. See...?

A bolt of lightning zigzagged down my spine. "Cici?"

"Yes, that's it. See See. Funny name. I told her that I didn't have a number, that you only call me. Well, I mean, I do know where you'll be staying in Sacramento, but I'd never tell anyone without your consent."

Cici. Why in the hell had I told her about Martha? I hung up the receiver, nearly breaking the hook with the force. I had an urge to rip out the entire box. Instead I chomped on a stick, a particularly poor substitute for a smoke right then.

~

One night in the Californian was enough. Fresno was a provincial outpost straining to be a city. Larger than Bakersfield, but only in size. New construction here and there, but without imagination, the kind that would soon decay. I'd planned to stay longer, but I saw no reason to do so now.

It was noon, Thursday, December 11th. I would drive straight through to Sacramento, arrive a day early, leaving time to ruminate, gather my strength. Maybe...maybe call Cici from there.

I asked the front desk clerk the location of the nearest grocery store. He directed me to the town's new Safeway, one block down on First Street.

~

EVERYTHING UNDER ONE ROOF. That's what the sign read, and it was only a slight exaggeration if your definition of everything is an endless maze of boxes and cans. Post-war plenty, brands too numerous to count. Fresh meats and produce anchored the store.

CEREALS. SOUPS. CONDIMENTS. I roamed the aisles with a shopping cart, a benefit since I'd left my cane in the car and stopped at SNACKS. This wasn't the time for anything fancy, or even nourishing. I needed bulk. I grabbed some pretzels and a bag of Crispy Potato Chips.

"*Crispy, crispy, to the very last bite, crispy, crispy, endless delight!*"

I trekked to the margins of the store for some bananas, a couple of apples and a pre-sliced block of American cheese. I thought about buying some walnuts from a large bin near the vegetable section, but I would have had to open them with my teeth. Still, I couldn't help but run my hands over the shells, enjoying the feel, divining something, guidance perhaps in the cool, hard ridges.

I picked up a carton of juice and a couple of Mars bars. On my way to the check out, I steered through FOREIGN FOODS, which was mostly Mexican fare. Beans, hot sauce, fixings for tacos. Cayenne and chile. It was one of the few sections of the store that didn't smell antiseptic. Of course, this was nothing compared to my father's place, which used to specialize in such things. Credit where credit is due, I suppose. His market was the real thing, not a shadow. The aisles were cluttered and narrow, the concrete floors stained from spills. The space was fragrant and alive. Then there was his imported Mexican chocolate, which drew fans from as far away as San Francisco.

"*Crispy, crispy, to the very last bite, crispy, crispy, endless delight!*" That damn jingle was lodged in my head now, the sweet children's voices belying the mercenary advertising strategy. Reminded me of a doctor's visit.

*"Do you really hear voices?" the doctor said.*
*"No. Not really. Just...my own thoughts."*
*"Well, that's fine. Haven't lost touch with reality, then."*
*"Is that good?"*
*"Of course. Better to be neurotic than psychotic."*
*I wondered.*

Near the cash register, there was a special on cherries. I didn't need them, but I couldn't resist. I loved the fruit, mostly because of James. Once when I was in my hideout, he'd brought a cherry pie for us to share. He was the only one who knew about that place and sensed I'd be there that day. It was my birthday and my father had forgotten, my thirteenth being the last he'd remembered. It shouldn't have mattered. I was sixteen, almost a man. But it did. James didn't let me brood, though. He made me laugh by stuttering out the Happy Birthday song. He brought some new girly magazines, and we thumbed through them as we ate the pie, the remains of which we left for the rats. After that, cherry pie became a tradition, and a code word for whatever we wanted it to mean.

I paid and hurried out. A few more clouds had shown up in my absence, but the air felt almost balmy, and the colorless street had suddenly taken on a note of the exotic. The sparse foliage looked lush, the drab concrete silvery.

The illusion was short lived, though. Soon Fresno returned to itself and I was eager to leave. I loaded the groceries into my car and headed west, back toward 99. Buildings thinned out and traffic started to clog. Brakes, slowing, flickering rear lights. Shit. And 99 was even worse. A bright line to nowhere.

I sucked on a stick and tried to clear my mind. I wanted to speed, past the crops, past my past, but I was blocked in. "Focus!" Think of the job. Something to hold on to. Something to be proud of.

*"Your mother would have been proud of you, Mijo."*

Where did that come from? When did my father say that? The year I made straight As? The time I won the reading award? I remember how odd it sounded, since he rarely mentioned her. He'd looked confused, too, as if the words had escaped from a locked diary. I clung to those words, though.

She was beautiful, he sometimes told me. *She loved you.* It was too painful to talk about, he said. If my grandmother even mentioned her name, he'd cut her off, too. *"Carlito, recuerdas cuando Isabella..."* Remember when Isabella ... .

It had nearly killed him. My mother's death at such a young age. So he'd blotted it out. With silence, with other women.

But now. Penny, goddamn you. Why couldn't you leave me to my story? So what if it was false. It was mine! That word went there, this one went here. Good enough. Easier to live with. I didn't ask for your version. All of the characters rewritten. Even my grandmother. She must have known, too. All that time. Together, she and my father.

*"Shh! Quiet, there's Andrés."*

That look on their faces. Plotting something. Caught in the act. I didn't know what it meant then. Now I understood. They'd made a decision. A dead mother was better than a cheat. But a lie like that required vigilance. *Shh!* I wondered. There must have been moments. Slips. Did they know what had become of her?

*"Slut," my father says under his breath.*

*"What's a slut, Pop?"*

*I'm about ten, waiting at a barbershop to get a haircut. My grandmother is sitting next to me. Pop's standing up, gazing out the window to our backs.*

*"What's a slut?" I say again.*

*"Never mind."*

*"A nasty girl," my grandmother says. "But don't look."*

*I try to obey but my head turns on its own. Nasty? That was what Pop called the cut on my hand. And the man who pulled down his pants at Griffith Park. All I see is a tired-looking woman wearing a lot of lipstick. She's leaning against a street lamp and smoking. Maybe that's it. Pop doesn't like smoking.*

*"I said don't look!" my grandmother repeats as she and my father whisper with their eyes.*

~

How hard it must have been. Keeping the secret. From neighbors, friends. Those candles on the mantel, the photograph of my parents' wedding. A rosary dangling on the frame. Poor Carlos. Poor Andrés. All for show. Makes sense that there was no funeral, that my mother wanted to be buried in Mexico. A burial too far for me to attend. Too far, too young.

~

Entering Madera County, traffic was still heavy. At one point it stopped entirely, so I reached into the grocery bag. What I really wanted was a drink, but I settled for some cherries and a Mars bar.

An hour crept by. My eyes were heavy. It was four o'clock, but it looked later. Thick grey had overtaken the waning blue. Up ahead, right off the road, was a partially lit up sign: HOT COFFEE. If it had been on the other side, I wouldn't have bothered. But it was right there. Plus, I needed to piss again.

The place was in the shape of a log cabin. Commercial and flimsy, crowded with frustrated drivers. NO PUBLIC TOILETS was written above the cash register. No tables or counter either. You stood, or took out. The line snaked around the unadorned interior. I took my spot, about ten customers back.

"The stars desert the skies...and rush to nestle in your eyes... It's magic..."

The voice was low, behind me.

"Without a golden wand, or mystic charms, fantastic things begin when I am in your arms..."

I swung around, coming face to face with the source. She smiled and began humming instead. Her tone was ethereal, reminding me of a thrush I'd once heard at the zoo.

"Didn't mean to startle you," she said, her wavy blonde hair falling loosely about a black turtleneck sweater.

I grunted out a response, gawking at her pin-up face. Right out of Hollywood. The kind soldiers kissed in their sleep.

"I really didn't mean to startle you," she said again, retying a peacock colored scarf around her slender waist. I love that song, don't you? Doris Day's version especially."

I shook my head, envisioning Day, with her scrubbed, medicinal look. Everyone said Day's voice was pure and clear, but it didn't appeal to me. This woman's was better. Richer. Day with a touch of loam.

"Well, to each his own. Have you read this?" she said, pointing to a book she was carrying.

The letters blurred as she drew closer, but the words included sex and ideal. "Can't say as I have."

She looked up at me, half-smiling.

I shook my head, strangely aroused.

She touched my jacket and then my cane. Her fingers were delicate, nails pink and manicured.

"Bum leg?" she said.

"Yeah."

"War?"

I wanted to say none of your business. Her questions were bold but somehow not impertinent.

"Childhood accident."

"Oh," she said, holding my gaze. "Anyone ever say you look like Gregory Peck?"

I shrugged.

"Especially in that movie with Ingrid Bergman. You know. *Spellbound*. He plays a man with amnesia. A real mental case. You're older than he was there, but yeah, you look like him all right."

Blood rushed to my face. Despite my complexion, it must have shown because she giggled. "Where ya headed?" she said.

"Up north," I answered, and turned to hide my arousal. But I sensed her energy. I thought I could hear her humming again, a sound that raised the hair on my arms. But when I turned, she wasn't there. I slumped, feeling...feeling what? Disappointed, dejected even. I placed my order and paid. Maybe she was outside. I pushed open the door. No. Just a greyer sky. I shook my head. And then I laughed. "You really are a mental case," I muttered, joining a couple of other men who were relieving themselves in a bush.

I sipped the coffee, which wasn't bad. As I approached my car, I noticed something on my windshield wiper. I plucked it off. It was a card, pink with black lettering that read: PRIVATE GENTLEMEN'S CLUB: DISCREET, ACCOMODATING, SANITARY.

I turned the card over. "Off at Oak. Two miles east. Right at Middlegrove. White farmhouse with an old swing out front. Ask for Roberta." The ink was fresh, the script round and inviting. "Ha." So that was it. A hooker. A slut! I laughed again. Probably her routine.

I tossed the card and got in the car. Roberta. The steering wheel was cold. Was I that easily taken in? I started the engine and turned on the heat, letting the warm air circulate. Something about her though. Audacious. And that voice.

Did she have any other flaws? My loins tingled at the thought. I envisioned the arch of her back, the young flesh released from the scarf. A scar, perhaps. A birthmark. Christ, maybe a disease. The club might be sanitary, but was she? Risky. Still, those strands of honey hair, the thought of them tickling my face, and elsewhere. Humming. Singing. Quick, unemotional. Not fraught, as with Cici. I got out of the car and nabbed the card.

~

My map showed the Oak exit. It was there, about three miles north. This wasn't my style, paying for sex. At least not for years. But I hadn't sought it out. It had come to me, one cripple to another, sensing my need.

Oak. There was the turnoff. A roughly paved road. "You speak and I hear violins. It's magic." Now I was singing the damn thing. Straight ahead, fields, a few cows. More clouds. Then a series of curves through a canopy of skeletal trees. Wet colored leaves carpeting the road.

The swing came into view before anything else. Rope and

wood, hanging from a tree, twitching a little with the breeze. Beyond that a chain-link fence and a shabby but massive two-story colonial. The farmhouse. Cock-a-doodle-doo.

I parked next to a couple of other cars, a refurbished Model T and a new Pontiac. Clients? I smoothed my hair, chewed an old piece of Wrigley's I found in the glove box and stashed the gun in my coat pocket. Just in case.

The muddy walkway was tracked with footprints. A sort of crime scene, of which my own pattern was now a part. I straightened myself and rang the bell. The chime was barely audible, but in short order, a woman resembling my high school librarian opened the door. Hands on her matronly hips, she eyed me through wire-framed glasses. "Yes?"

"I...I...was sent by Roberta," I said, sounding like James.

"Card?" she said, as if I were checking out a book.

I handed it over.

"Just a minute," she said and closed the door.

She returned and showed me into a waiting area with a squat Christmas tree and Victorian furnishings. Worn velvet and lace. Scratched, polished wood. A dusty glass cabinet filled with miniature porcelain shoes. Tired respectability, unremarkable if not for the reek of debauchery.

"I'm Hazel. Please," she said, pointing to a wingback chair with a greasy-looking doily.

I sat, listening for the thrush but hearing nothing. "So," I said. "Roberta?"

She frowned at me over her glasses. "Roberta was a scout."

"Yes," I said. "It worked. So may I see her now? And how much?"

"When I say scout, I mean, that's her job where you're concerned. Her only job."

"What do you mean?"

"You didn't think you were actually going to *be* with her, did you?"

"What? Of course I did. Why not?"

"We've got rules. Standards."

"*Here*? What kind?"

"About who can, well, have relations with whom," Hazel said, suddenly mutating from librarian to prison guard. "Surely you understand. No race mixing. But don't worry. We've got just the woman for you. Rosa. What a beauty. And she's in high demand. Or Mariana. Also lovely. You'll see. They'll be down in a minute."

"Are you kidding? I'll pay for and screw who I want!"

"I'm sorry," she said matter-of-factly. "This is my place of business and I make the rules."

I laughed, a deep, guttural laugh that I didn't recognize. Standards? She ran a damn whorehouse. Illegal, even out here. I should have turned her in. I thought about searching the rooms.

Then, footsteps. I turned to the sound and witnessed a hefty, cowboy type buckling his belt. "See you next time," he said, to a robed Negro girl standing in the doorway. He then hurried down past me, rattling the entire house as he went. The girl waved and returned to the room.

"So, do you want to meet the *chicas* or not?" Hazel said.

"Wait. Wait a minute. You don't call *that* race mixing?" I said.

"There are exceptions."

Hazel must have taken my silence for agreement because the *chicas* were on their way. I could hear them fluttering, jingling. In seconds, they were parading in front of me. And they were indeed lovely. Dark and ripe, at the height of the season. Rosa, the taller one, was dressed in black. Mariana, short and compact, was in white. They strutted and turned, showing off their wares.

"Two for the price of one," Hazel said. "For your trouble."

An insult to the women, and for a moment I felt defensive,

even protective. But the feeling passed. They knew what they were doing. And I didn't have time to argue. I was here, in need of release. So I followed them, to a stuffy room in the back of the house.

A giant bed stretched from one wall to the other. I sat on it. Mariana motioned to Rosa who sat beside me and touched my leg. My bad leg, as if that would help. I drew her towards me, running the back of my hand on her cheek. It was smooth and taut. Then I looked over at Mariana.

"Come on," Rosa said to her.

Mariana obeyed, inching closer with a kind of floating gait. Her hair was black and wavy. She grinned and reached out. I lifted my arms. Trying to warm to her, hoping to rise like my grandmother's bread. "Come," I said, "over here," patting my good knee. Her eyes glistened.

She sat, smelling of creams, potions and cigarettes.

"*Cariño*," she said, getting closer.

She smelled of something else, too. Something too familiar. Too close to home.

"*Cariño*," she said again.

My mother must have come on to men like that. Same fake term of endearment. I gagged and pushed the girl off my knee.

"*¿Qué pasa?*" she said. "Do you not like me?"

No. I do not. You're a disgrace. *Puta!* But all I said was: "You should go home."

I put a twenty-dollar bill in her hand and got out of there before Hazel noticed, swearing that one day I'd come back, with a warrant for Roberta.

# 15

## COMMAND POST

I was back on the road, still creeping along, desire replaced with a revulsion I couldn't shake. Sleazy broads. Just kids really. Sickening to think of my mother, my own mother.

I rolled down the car window, letting in the frigid air. The wind whipped around, rattling the grocery bags. It felt good for about a minute. I rolled it back up and turned on the radio. A noisy void.

I snacked on a Mars bar and drove, although walking, even with my cane, would have been faster at this rate. Making matters worse, a couple of cars that had apparently collided had pulled to the side. No one seemed to be hurt, but it was still a show that further slowed things down.

A mile or two ahead, almost *in* the road, someone was standing. I squinted. A man, leaning on a car with an outstretched thumb. He was animated, flagging everyone that passed. I inched by him with no intention of stopping. I never picked up hitchhikers. But he gave me pause. This was no sailor or hobo. He was dressed-up, and his car looked like a new model Cadillac. His image was fleeting, but there was an elegance about him. It was an impulse, probably a bad one, but I pulled over, turned off the engine and exited on the passenger side.

"Oh, thank God," he said, watching me approach.

He was dressed-up all right. In a tux. Thick, brown hair, with a Clark Gable mustache.

"I'm Todd," he said, extending his gloved hand.

"Andrew. What's the problem?" I said.

"I have no idea. The thing just stopped."

"Gas?"

"Yes. Just gassed up in Fresno. I must be driving the Titanic. Car's brand new. Not supposed to break down."

"Bad luck."

"I don't even know how to change a tire," he said.

I wasn't surprised. "I only know the basics," I said. "But I can check under the hood if you want."

"Oh, yes, please. I'm due at my brother's wedding in Modesto. Best man, you know."

I looked under the hood and asked him to try to start the engine. It turned over but wouldn't catch. I took off the air filter and looked at the carburetor. "Todd, pump the gas a couple of times while you're turning it over."

Dry as a bone.

"I'd guess a busted fuel pump," I said, "but I don't really know. I can drive you to a phone booth. You'll probably have to have it towed."

"I'd appreciate that. But, uh, where are you headed?"

I thought about lying. "Sacramento."

I knew what was next. I'd set myself up for it. But now, I realized.... He was a little too coiffed. And his voice had an effeminate lilt.

"I know I'm asking a lot, but would you mind dropping me in Modesto? It's on your way, and I'm in a real bind here."

Shit. Well, I had to now. I'd throw him out if he tried anything. Heard stories about these guys.

"All right. But I've got to get going."

"Bless you," he said, and locked up his car.

Once on the road, we didn't talk at first. His cologne was strong, so I kept the window open.

"Too cold?" I finally said.

"Whatever you like is fine."

"What do you do?" he asked.

"Lawyer. You?"

"Architect."

He went quiet, which was fine. It was getting dark, so I turned on my headlights. Fog and dust swirled in the glare. A varmint of some sort came out of nowhere. I tapped the breaks, and it scurried off.

"Hope it made it," he said.

"Yeah."

"I'm quite fond of animals. More honest than humans. And they don't talk back."

"You'd be surprised. I have a parrot. That's all he does."

He giggled, girlishly. "What's his name?"

"Emerson. Have a pet?"

"A dog. Ulysses."

We stopped for him to call a tow truck and a friend to pick him up in Modesto. Then, we drove on. I relaxed somewhat. He was all right, as long as he kept his distance.

Indeed, he was close enough with that cologne. I'd probably smell of it for days. It had a citrusy fragrance, syrupy, like an overripe orange. That may have been what made me think of my father again. Oranges. The smell never left him. But that's where the comparison stopped because this guy obviously swung the other way. Worst thing that could happen to a man, the ultimate assault to machismo. Or so my father believed, and I guessed I did as well. So you could imagine my reaction when he once accused James and me of the behavior. I laughed and then punched him in the gut, which reassured him. I guessed true friendship was something he'd never experienced. Couldn't imagine love without sex. After James died, I couldn't either. But sex without love was another matter. *That* I was good at. Even the kind I'd just fled. Like I said, it was a long time ago. Long before I knew about my mother, when I thought she was only dead ...

~

*Hot summer night. I'm seventeen, sitting on the porch, shirtless and miserable. As usual, my father's not home. My grandmother calls me into her room. Her rheumatism is acting up, so she's in bed early. I don't want to go, but I do. She's my grandmother.*

*I open the screen door. A mosquito flies in. So many of them this year. Guarantee one finds its way to me tonight, sucks my blood and leaves me a giant welt. I'm too sweet, my grandmother says.*

*I stand in the doorway of her room. It's stifling. She's always cold. She motions for me to come close. Her long, thick hair, usually pulled up in a bun, lays on the pink pillowcase in wavy grey strands. The room smells of camphor and incense. She's in a housedress and a sweater! She sits up, moaning a little, but smiles. One of her back teeth is missing, and, just now, the vacancy nearly brings me to tears.*

*"Andrés, did you eat something?"*

*"Yeah."*

*"What?"*

*"Some of your cold soup."*

*"Was it good?"*

*I nod.*

*"What are you going to do tonight?"*

*"Nothing."*

*"What's wrong?"*

*"Nothing."*

*She knows that's not true. But she also knows better than to probe.*

*"Can you rub my shoulders a little, Mijo?"*

*I sigh. No, I want to say. But I do it, as I've done since I was little. Back then there was more flesh, although never as firm as the kids' mothers at school. Now, she's bony, and her skin is paper-thin. She bruises easily, so I have to be careful.*

*"Bueno, Mijo. Gracias."*

*When I feel her begin to relax I know sleep is near. She scoots down and asks me to turn off the light. I start to walk out, past the rocking chair with the hand-knitted blanket, past the makeshift altar to the Virgin of Guadalupe.*

*"Andrés," she calls out. "When I die I will still protect you. I'll be your guardian. Look for me in the wind."*

*Back on the porch, I'm alone, feeling on the brink of an episode. James stops by. He always tells me that he can read my mood by my posture, and that night is alarmed, for he says I'm fully contracted, like his pet turtle the day he discovered her dead.*

*I order him to leave. As usual, he ignores me. "Cherry pie," he says, hoping to make me laugh. Pacing, smoking, and yammering on about turtles, how their shells were originally designed for burrowing rather than protection. But that night I don't want any of it. I take offense at the turtle comparison and balk at what he calls his "brilliant fucking idea." And he means that literally. The fucking part, anyway. Doesn't he know me better than that? But James is certain he's right. "You need to get out of yourself." Or actually, "you n...n need to g...get ou...out of your s...self." His damn stutter. That's what makes me give in, makes it hard to pity myself.*

*Thing is, I'm not a virgin. Girls like me, always have. And the feeling is mutual. But I hate their expectations. Holding hands, wearing my ring. Phone calls, flowers. I'm troubled, the kind of boy girls long to mother, particularly when they learn my own mother is dead.*

*James drives me to a brothel in the Hollywood hills, where the only expectation is desire. Of course, I know of such places. Not only from hearsay, not only from books and movies and police raids covered in the news, but from my father, who frequented them in his own youth and even promised a future father-son visit.*

*Future. Soon. One day. Like everything else.*

*James is right. I take an instant liking to an experienced señorita who knows how to make me feel wanted. Like a man not a boy. For the moment. The place is just what I need. Secluded. Dense with chaparral, the broken HOLLYWOODLAND sign a fitting backdrop. Booze and perfume. Jazz. Curtains of glittery beads. A den of iniquity, but a tasteful one. Behind those beads, a refuge. Cherry Pie.*

~

I pulled off at the Modesto exit. Todd's cousin was meeting him there. He got out and leaned his head in through the car window. "Thank you, again," he said, handing me a business card. "If you ever need anything."

I exhaled. Another card. He was nice enough, but I was glad to be rid of him. There was a rest stop nearby. I parked and shut my eyes. Just for a minute. I needed to snooze. When I awoke, it was three o'clock.

The road was now empty. I was revived, but so was my leg. It was in transition, that uneasy state where it could go either way. Nerves, maybe. All alone out here. Blacker than oil. Still, it was pushing the gas pedal, modulating the pressure. The sensation was nothing new, of course, but it seemed stranger somehow. Even less under my control than usual. A spirit, giving it commands, ensuring I wouldn't crash. Outside, the wind was howling. *Abuela? Is that you?*

~

The early morning sun poked through the lingering grey. My eyes burned, and the dreary flat farmland offered little visual relief. Yet I felt a touch of exhilaration. I'd made it. Sacramento was straight ahead, situated at the confluence of two rivers, the American and the Sacramento, the one for which the city was named. I couldn't see them from here, but I knew of their force. Massive floods on the one hand, vital sources of commerce on the other. Like most things, neither all good nor all bad. Still, the thought of all that water made me well up. As if I'd awakened from a coma to a bowl of my grandmother's albondigas soup, the tears nearly as soothing. The entire trip had been a kind of dream. A dream within a dream. But now I'd reached my destination. This was a city built on a near perfect grid. No blurred lines. No murky borders. A place where real things happened. Where I was going to make something happen.

I took the downtown exit, passing tree-lined streets with small bungalows. At a stoplight, I squinted, trying to peer into a window, but all I could make out was the reflection of the yard's canopy of oaks, still showing the last gasp of fall.

I was heading to the Senator Hotel on the corner of 12th and L, across from State Capitol Park, in the center of the grid. The town was as easy to navigate as it appeared on the map.

The U.S. and California flags waved over the hotel. I drove up to the entrance, handed my keys to the valet and checked in.

The Italianesque building was actually divided in two, connected by an ornate, sky lit lobby.

"You're on the fifth floor," the Negro bellman said in the elevator. "Nice view of the capitol but part of it's under construction. The apse."

"The what?"

"Apse. Roundish thing," he said, with a laugh. "It was demolished to make way for an expansion. But nothing's replaced it yet."

"That's okay," I said, and gave him a good tip.

The room was clean and elegant, with mahogany furniture, brass fixtures and peach-colored linens. I took a shower and fell into a deep sleep, waking three hours later still upbeat. So much so, that I intentionally left my cane in the room and took the stairs down to the lounge, also decorated in mahogany, brass and peach. I picked up a free copy of the Sacramento Bee, ordered a hamburger and a rum toddy, and sat down in a plush velvet chair. RAIN IS OVER; SKIES WILL BE FAIR TOMORROW, the headline read. I let the corners of my mouth turn up. A roaring fire was burning in a stone hearth. Having come through a fire of my own, I felt at liberty to enjoy it.

I walked outside, nodding in the holiday spirit. The air was fresh, scented with pine. I started for the park, but then stopped. What was I waiting for? Now was the time, when I was feeling strong. I headed back to my room and placed a call to John. If all seemed well, I'd follow with one to Cici, on her private line.

~

"Andy. That you?"

"I'm here. Arrived early."

"Oh, good, good. How was the trip?"

"Just fine," I said.

There was no response. He was smoking. I could hear his inhale, deeper than regular breath. Finally, I broke the silence.

"Any news?"

"Status quo. The men are anxious to meet you."

"And I them."

"Uh, huh."

"John, you sound, I don't know, a little distracted." I eyed my cane. "Cici okay?"

"Cici? She's visiting her cousin in New York. Damn lonely without her."

New York? That was good, I supposed. "For how long?"

"That's the problem. Not sure. Ruth is sick. Cici's helping her out until she's better. I'd fly out there but my second-in-command just retired. Plus Ruth never liked me. I wouldn't want to upset her."

"Ruth?"

"The cousin."

I couldn't imagine Cici playing nurse, but I was relieved.

"I don't know how you do it," John said. "The single life's not for me."

"I've got my bird."

He laughed. And I relaxed. Whatever Cici had called about must not have been that important. "Hope it all goes well," I said, almost giddy.

"And for you, too, Andy. Tomorrow's the big day."

# 16

## DEPLOYMENT

The meeting place reminded me of my house in Boyle Heights, absent the negative associations. Modest, tidy, decorated for Hanukkah instead of Christmas. It was west of downtown and belonged to one of the men. As soon as I arrived, I was whisked downstairs, past a menorah and tinseled Star of David, into a windowless, sparsely furnished basement. The group was waiting. Seven members of varying ages, dressed not in Hassidic but everyday garb.

"Welcome, Mr. Martin." The man who spoke was stooped, but the gleam in his eyes suggested a hidden power. "I'm Hiram," he said, in perfect English, meaning he must not have been one of the members who, as John said, had been in the camps. The rest of the men then encircled me and one by one offered their hand. Rough, soft, large, small, calloused, sweaty, bony. Each was different, but united in purpose. Most of them wore long-sleeve shirts, but as we shook, I glanced at their arms anyway, dreading the numbers, the dark code to their motivation. They all glanced at my cane, perhaps for the same reason.

On a card table were sandwiches and Cokes.

"Grab some food and make yourself comfortable," Hiram

said. "My wife was going to prepare something more elaborate, but our daughter needed a babysitter. So salami and cheese it is. No time to keep kosher."

"Was your drive up here okay?" one of the men said.

I swallowed. "Yes."

Hiram watched me eat. "How long did it take you?"

Years, I wanted to say. "Just a few days."

"Hotel okay?"

"Yes."

"Excellent."

We ate for a while. The men caught up on birthdays and funerals. They laughed, talked about which wife made the best *latkes*.

After twenty minutes or so, Hiram said: "John has vouched for you, of course."

I nodded, guessing the small talk was over.

"You know, we were a little hesitant when he first recommended you. You're not exactly one of us," he said, in a half-joking tone.

"No."

"And not because you're not a Jew."

I thought of my leg. "Oh?"

He turned to the other men, who had stopped eating, and then looked back at me. "I could be diplomatic, Andrew, but the situation calls for bluntness. It's your disloyalty to your own people that gave us pause. That is, in the courtroom. We tracked your cases."

Quite a presumption, though not unfamiliar. "I'm not disloyal," I said. "I'm a lawyer." He wanted more, but I wasn't here for that. I went silent.

"It doesn't matter, really," he finally said, smiling. "I don't think you share our politics either."

"Maybe not. But we're united in our antipathy to Nazis, to anti-Semitism."

He nodded, seeming to like that response. "Like Gregory Peck in *Gentlemen's Agreement*."

"Ha. Good movie." Even you? I thought.

"We do want to make sure you understand the significance of this mission."

"I think I do," I said.

"Beyond the obvious hypocrisy of hiring a former enemy, I mean. Because that's done all the time."

"I would assume that it's the nature of the enemy."

"Yes. It's personal for us. We all lost family members in the camps. But it's also our deep concern about this country. I'm a natural-born citizen, a few of us aren't. But now more than ever, we believe in a transparent government. After Germany, there's no other way. The public should know what its officials are up to."

"I agree," I said, and I really did.

"Good. Well, let's get to it, then. Wolf?"

A fellow about my age with a neat goatee and angular features rose from the couch and pulled down a screen from the wall. That's when I noticed the projector. And it's also when I spotted the code, imprinted on the inside of his left forearm where his sleeve had been rolled up. Though I'd seen the photos, the reality gave me a start. I turned away, as if I'd walked in on him naked. He waited until I was seated and then, with the accent Hiram lacked, asked for the lights to be dimmed.

"Mr. Martin," Wolf said.

"Andrew, please."

"Andrew. So, here is where Joseph Reynolds lives. That's his alias, we think. We've yet to discover his real name, one of the things you might help us with."

Naturally.

The projector clicked on, the reel turned as I gazed at a single story tract home with a picket fence and grassy yard. The camera panned all around, the neighboring houses, a few cars on the street, a walkway.

"It's rather secluded, in an enclave near the American River, which makes filming challenging. But we've been patient."

The grainy, black and white image had the effect of a newsreel, intensifying the import. The house. The man. The supposed Nazi. The believed-to-be-spy.

"And there he is," Wolf said.

I leaned in. Fair, wiry, with a high forehead, the kind phrenologists associate with intelligence. He was watering his lawn. In his short-sleeved tee shirt and dungarees, he looked every bit an American suburbanite.

"That was taken last summer. A hundred degrees that day. We watched him for hours. He barely broke a sweat."

I stood up and got closer to the screen. The man, Joseph, turned and aimed the hose at a flowerbed. From that angle, I could see that his shirt had some writing on it. SACRAMENTO STATE COLLEGE.

"It's not just for show," Hiram said. "We know John has informed you about Reynolds' union involvement. But he also works at the college. In maintenance. A jack-of-all-trades."

"I didn't even know there was a state branch up here," I said.

"Only two years old. Right now it rents space from the junior college. And it's fitting that he works there. Charles Goethe founded it. The eugenicist. Getty, they call him up here. The one that influenced Hitler. At least that what they claimed at Nuremberg. You know, the one that hates your folk as much as ours."

I felt a little sheepish. I should have known more about Goethe and his ilk. There was that business in L.A. in the twenties. The plague that hit that Mexican neighborhood. City elders blamed the inhabitants. Not their living conditions, but something innate in their blood. Like rats. The houses were razed. That incident burned in my father's soul. He never forgot it. As for me, it was easier to feel outrage over the treatment of other minorities. Jews, blacks, Japanese, anyone other than my own people. I suppose because of what happened to James. Because being a Mexican was more important to my father than being a father. There were reasons, and even now I felt that wall go up.

"The college isn't much to look at, but might be a place to start."

"How certain are you that this is really another Mengele and not some *average* Joe?" I said.

The men snickered. "Ninety percent, but that's why we've hired you, of course."

The small-handed man spoke up. "I'm a scientist," he said, his accent lighter than Wolf's. "I escaped right before the war. Reynolds worked at my institution, I'm almost certain. I didn't know him, but I remember his face. His and a number of others whose identity was kept secret, due, we were told, to the sensitive nature of their project." He shook his head. "I didn't question it then. Still don't know exactly what they were up to, although it's not hard to imagine."

"Indeed," Hiram said. "Another group member who is not here today is convinced he saw Joe at the Dachau infirmary. Didn't know his name, but said he was doing testing of some sort, with tubes full of blood. And there are other corroborating witnesses."

"How did you trace him here?" I said.

"We have a network, of course. Devoted people who keep track of such things. But we have to be absolutely certain. Ninety per cent isn't good enough."

The room was stuffy. Cigarette smoke curled in the projector light, creating the aura of an interrogation room. I grabbed another coke as the camera panned to the porch. Out of the front door, a woman appeared, carrying a water glass.

"This is his wife," Wolf said. "We don't know much about her, but the relationship seems genuine. As you know, she's pregnant. Quite pregnant. Reynolds calls her Claire."

I studied her as she handed her husband the beverage. Light-haired, plump, probably even without her belly. She wore a patterned smock and smiled as her husband drank. Her face was broad, but, for a moment, Cici clouded my view.

The film stopped, the screen went white.

"So," Hiram said, turning on the lights. "Now you've seen him. Any questions?"

Thousands, but only one for Hiram. "What next?"

"You know where he is likely to be. Home, union meetings, college. How you get the evidence is up to you. But we need evidence. Hard evidence. Something tangible."

"What does that mean, exactly?"

"Something that will pique the interest of the press."

"The holidays might be tricky," Wolf said, "but we can't wait. We don't know when he might leave again. Here are the addresses you'll need," he said, handing me a folder. "There's a photo of him and his wife in there, too."

I took the folder, skimming it against Wolf's tattoo as I did. He must have seen me avert my eyes because he said: "It's okay. You can look."

I wanted to. And yet I felt afraid, like a kid forced to look under the bed at night. He brought his arm closer. 20405. Twenty thousand, four hundred and five. Behind those impossible numbers were trains and showers, ovens and gas. Swastikas, salutes, and yellow badges. Mountains of decaying flesh. Horrors I might have been forced to see for myself had *my* number not been 4-F.

"At first they used a metal stamp," Wolf said. "All the numbers punched in with one blow on the chest. Ink rubbed into the bleeding wound. I was one of the lucky ones. A single needle on the arm, with indelible ink."

Words ran through my brain, but they were all inadequate. So I just shook my head.

Wolf continued: "Jewish law forbids tattooing."

"I think God forgives us on that score," Hiram said.

"Yeah. If there is a god."

This time I nodded.

Hiram stood up, as did the others. "It goes without saying how grateful we are."

"I haven't done anything yet."

"You're here. That's half the battle."

I nodded again. *Righter than you know.*

"I've included a phone number. Contact me there when you've got the goods," Hiram said. "Or if there's a problem."

"All right."

"Any other questions?"

"John said you might want to arm me. I don't think that's necessary," I said, knowing that I had a gun anyway. "We can turn it over to the cops if it gets that far."

"Agreed. Anything else?"

Is this a dream? I wanted to say, but just answered: "No."

~

Back in my hotel room, a couple of shots of rum under my belt, I planned the next day. First, I'd go to the college. Christmas was a week away. The students were presumably on break. But maintenance didn't rest. I remembered that from USC. No matter how empty the campus was, grass was cut, windows washed, trash collected. Things needed to be maintained. Hiram said that Joe was a jack-of-all trades, so I'd wander around, see if I could catch him trading. Try to figure out what he was getting in return. Next, I'd check out the union hall. The address listed in the folder was on Broadway, close to the hotel. I could walk there. Unlikely there would be a meeting before Christmas, but something might strike me. Same with the house. Except I'd drive there.

I was lying on my side. The bed was a little too soft for my liking, but big enough to stretch out my legs. No trouble with the limb today. My energy had become focused, contained. One foot, one leg, in front of the other. I felt strong. Strong enough to fight back anyone that would try to take me off course. Cici. Penny. Father. Mother.

I turned on my back and gazed at the ceiling, like I used to do as kid. Back then the white stucco served as a canvas, open to infinite meaning. On good days, populated with friends and animals, mountains and oceans. On bad days, a deserted town, a land without hope. The plaster here was smoother, cleaner. Except for a long, fine crack, probably from an earthquake. We had several such fissures in our home. Every Californian did. Damn Mother Nature. Any minute another could hit.

You never knew how long the shaking would last, how intense it would be. I remember the day my father had me committed, after I'd accused him of complicity in James' death. There was a quake that morning. Only a small tremor, lasting a few seconds. But for me it never stopped, ushered in a tsunami.

I'd screamed at him, said I wished it were he who had been killed.

*"You've lost all reason, Mijo! You wouldn't say any of this if you were thinking clearly. We have to get your head straight."*

The worst part was that he used my history, my fragile psyche, to stifle me. He knew. Over and over again he'd heard the doctors say I'd grow out of it, that problems were common for a child without a mother. But he wouldn't have it any other way.

Pop wanted the "accident" to blow over, had me committed so that people wouldn't hear my accusations. Or if they did, wouldn't believe them. It was he, not I, who wasn't thinking clearly, who was so devoted to his so-called higher purpose that he was willing to sacrifice his son. My hospital stay that time was short, however, because even the doctors could see that my reasoning was just fine. And I'd left with a long-term goal: to undo and rebuild, to become my father's antithesis. I was focused then, too. Even after he was killed in prison two months later. Indeed, even more so then.

~

It was the tattoo that had persuaded me to give myself over, to let go of the lingering doubt about the mission. In the face of those grim numbers, doubt fled, like a vampire at the sight of a crucifix.

I held out my own arms. My hands, large and sinewy, black hair on the knuckles, were steady. A raised vein ran the length of both forearms. For someone who didn't regularly lift weights, my biceps were fairly developed. I flexed, felt one and then the other.

Still hard as brick. And my skin was tough and thick. Caramel in hue just now, my winter white. In the summer, the color deepened to a Hershey bar. Very few moles, and the ones I had were flat and tiny. Flecks, Cici had called them. Little nuggets. Leftovers from the gold rush, when my ancestors, the Californios, called the land theirs.

My father, however, had moles and scars and a tattoo of his own. A sacred heart, right on his ass, where no one except his whores could see it. Bulbous and red, it scared me, too. As a kid, I feared it might start beating at any moment. He laughed when I told him that, said it symbolized his love for his people, although the location made me wonder. A source of pride, he'd say, a permanent mark of their survival. Perhaps in a perverse way, Wolf viewed his the same.

## 17

## RECONNAISSANCE

December 23rd, nine o'clock, bitter cold. L.A. was twenty degrees warmer, and I started to wish I were there. Nearly two weeks, and I'd yet to glimpse Joe.

I'd been to the campus five days straight. Nothing much to look at. Concrete blocks for classrooms, the worst of modern design. Austere, and dreary without students. The only workers I'd observed were Mexican. One was plucking weeds, another sweeping a sidewalk, another erasing an enormous KILROY WAS HERE sign, chalked onto a wall. I wondered whether Goethe himself had a hand in the hiring, although manual labor certainly didn't preclude spreading disease.

I sipped the orange juice that room service had just delivered. It was fresh and full of pulp. I devoured the bacon and cut into the special capitol French toast, a thick wedge of egg-soaked bread, fried to perfection, planted with a dollhouse California flag.

I'd gone to the union hall. It was a beautiful, old brick structure with stained glass windows and a grand wooden door. The year 1850 was engraved over the entrance. Weighty and ivy covered, the building oozed history. Labor history. Strikes. Some valid, some not, but all inspired by the Democratic party's belief in the right to organize. It might seem surprising that I support that right when there is true abuse. When workers are put in danger, for example, because of shoddy equipment. But I've seen too many businesses irreparably hurt by frivolous demands, usually involving more money. Am I biased? Of course. When business suffers, I suffer. To me, strikes should be the last, not the first, resort. Unlike my father, who never saw a strike he didn't like. Union halls were like churches to him, holy places where authority wasn't to be questioned.

As I'd anticipated, the place was closed, shut with a hefty padlock. For renovations, a sign said, with the reopening scheduled for the summer. NEXT MEETING TO BE DETERMINED. So Joe, and any Reds he might have cozied up to, wouldn't be there for a while. They might be convening elsewhere, but as Wolf said, we had to act now. I contacted Hiram to see if he knew anything, but he didn't.

I feared that the house might be a dead end, too. Fitting, given that it was on a cul-de-sac. I'd driven by several times, camera in tow, sometimes parking on the other side of the street. But I never saw Joe, nor his wife, Claire. The house had a large, rectangular window, but the curtains were always drawn. Yet, lamps were on at night and smoke billowed from the chimney.

Last night I'd parked closer than usual, in a spot where Christmas lights from a neighbor's house illuminated the wet street. Red, green, blue, gold. The colors glimmered blurrily, like underwater jewels. I was gazing at them, mesmerized by their kaleidoscope effect, when a stark brightness forced me to squint. Headlights. And the car pulled right into Joe's driveway. I slid down and peered over the steering wheel.

A man got out. Even from where I was, I could see that he was rotund, bald and dressed in white. Not a dinner jacket. A doctor's coat. I could recognize the shape of that cloth in my sleep. And he carried the telltale bag.

My mind raced through the possibilities, the most obvious being that Claire was in labor. But maybe it was Joe's contact. Maybe he was in disguise. Maybe even another Nazi. I snuck out and examined the car. A Packard. Older model. Well-kept. The door wasn't locked, a sign of either innocence or carelessness, so with one eye on the house, I opened it and flicked on my flashlight. Immaculate. Nothing in the back or front. Not even a gum wrapper. It smelled of leather and alcohol, but not the drinking kind. I pressed the glove box. Empty, except for the registration. I perused the entirely normal looking document. The owner was indeed a physician. Melvin Sharp, MD. I took down the license plate number just in case and returned to my car. Within ten minutes, the man came back out, said something I couldn't hear, and left.

I waited another half hour, until the house went dark. When I got back to the hotel, I checked the Yellow Pages. Melvin Sharp. "Sacramento's most trusted gynecologist." Twenty years in practice. A photo of the doctor—bald, double-chinned—confirmed his identity. "Office or house calls, patient convenience is our motto." I put two and two together and in this case decided it was probably four. A check-up, maybe a false alarm. At least I knew someone was home. Most likely Claire. But was Joe?

~

The phone rang. I tensed, fearing bad news.
"Yes?"
"Mr. Martin, a package came for you. Would you like a bellman to bring it up?"
I exhaled. I knew what it was, an overcoat I'd purchased

from Macy's. I'd dreaded fighting the holiday shoppers, but I was tired of being cold. My skin might be tough, but it was used to a temperate climate. As it turned out, the crowds weren't so bad, and I soon found a grey wool herringbone that fit. The coat was stylish, but subdued and respectable. There was a small tear at the cuff, however, which the salesman offered to have fixed.

"No thanks," I said. "I'll come down."

The lobby was abuzz. Guests were arriving, laden with festively wrapped presents. A couple of human elves manned a garlanded table, giving away coffee and hot chocolate. The holiday spirit was on full display, everyone in the here and now, forgetting about yesterday and tomorrow.

Except for me. Suddenly, I was thinking of both, of Christmas past and future. The Christmas Eve before James died in particular, when he'd come over for my grandmother's tamales. James, who despite claiming to hate the season, always gave of himself. He couldn't say enough about the meal that night, licking his fingers in an exaggerated show of appreciation. And then, with Louis Prima on the record player, he asked my grandmother to dance. She was hesitant, embarrassed, but as the evening wore on, her wrinkles seemed to fade, her arthritic steps turned fluid.

Then, of course, there was that Christmas I'd spent at the hospital, alone and suffering, without a visit from my father. I could still taste the slimy, green gelatin they passed off as dessert. I could feel the straightjacket-like sheets, too, hear the man in the next room howling like a trapped animal. Not to mention those well-meaning carolers, bringing tidings of insufferable joy. If it hadn't been for James, sending me a cherry pie, I might have used one of those sheets as a noose.

And next year? Would there be something to celebrate? Would I see the world anew? Run free, healed, caneless? Or would I be back at the cemetery, limping passed the gravestones, mourning my defeat? Alive, but seeing my own name among the dead.

~

"I was told there was package for me," I said to the concierge.

"Yes, Mr. Martin. Here you go," he said, handing me a jewelry sized box.

"That's not mine."

He leaned over my shoulder. "Says Andrew Martin."

It did. I'd had my mail forwarded here. But the postmark... New York. I ripped it open. Inside the box was a half sheet of paper, blank on one side, writing on the other. I looked around for a chair and sat down. I fingered the card, eyeing the wastebasket right next to me. Easiest thing in the world to toss it out of existence. But I turned it over. "Call me," it said, followed by an out of state phone number in Cici's unmistakable scrawl.

So, she was back at it. Her cousin was probably better. Maybe she was bored. But how did she know I was here? Not from Martha. John? He missed her. She probably twisted it out of him.

The paper was yellow, a smudge of lipstick on the corner. Her own stationary was white, imprinted with her initials. She liked sending cards, letters, little notes, even though I'd repeatedly warned her of the danger. One time, she sent a telegram through a courier who had the temerity to interrupt me in court with it. I was furious, but the message was cryptic enough to make me worry. So much so that I asked for a recess and ran to the phone. And what was so urgent? What did she want? To hear my voice. Just to hear my damn voice.

I thought of that incident, a few others, too. Cici could be impulsive. We'd talked about that. How she could get caught up in a moment, an emotion, and then forget all about it a day later.

She might have already been regretting sending me the message. Maybe it was something more, but I tried to put the brakes on my worry. Even if she were testing me, she would eventually tire of the effort.

"Oh, Mr. Martin! There *is* another package for you," the man said, handing me a large box. "Is this what you were expecting?"

"Yes, I think so." I took out the coat. It was soft and warm and mended. I tossed out both boxes and stuffed the note in my new pocket. Deep, where it would be hard to find.

~

With the coat buttoned, forty-seven degrees almost felt balmy. It was nearing eleven o'clock, and I was on the campus again. The wind was whipping brown leaves across an otherwise stilled scene. I peeked into a few classrooms, devoid of anything but desks and chalkboards. I tapped my cane on the cement walkway, hearing a faint echo.

There was a football field, the grass sparse, and a scoreboard against which a tall ladder leaned. I walked over and sat down on the first row of bleachers, imagining a cheering crowd. Before 4-F I'd been good at sports. I was coordinated, had natural ability, one of the best players on my Little League team. Yeah, Little League. I'd joined, even though there, too, I was an outsider. The other players admired my talent, but from afar. I remember one day, when my diving catch won the game.

*"Good job, Martínez," the coach says.*
*"Thanks."*
*"Nice catch," the team members echo.*
*I nod, waiting for the slap on the back, an offer to join them for a milkshake. I wouldn't have gone, but it hurts that I'm not asked.*

*I turn to the stands. Why I don't know. My father has never come before. Too busy. And he's not there now. But there are other parents, fathers and mothers, searching for their sons, no matter if they won or lost.*

*I go home, rip off my uniform and brood. My grandmother knocks on my door, asks about the game. I tell her to leave me alone. And something else. For the first time, I think of battle. Of fighting. Of wearing a more somber uniform. The idea that I will one day serve in the army strangely calms me. More than that, it fills me with a kind of euphoria, as if I've suddenly discovered the meaning of life. The feeling doesn't last, but the idea does.*

~

I could throw a football farther than anyone at high school. Coaches tried to recruit me. But I was a weird kid, too sensitive, not predictable or dedicated enough. Everyone knew I saw a shrink and that I was absent more than other kids. Missing school was one thing, but doing so for psycho reasons was something else. An omen, I guess, of the army's eventual rejection.

The coat was doing its job, but the wind was biting my face. I pulled up the collar and looked around. Beyond the field to the left were the classrooms, to the right the parking lot, where my car sat alone. I walked back through the halls, looking around this corner and that, following phantoms.

By noon I was deflated. And hungry. But the sun had emerged, so I went back to the bleachers to eat the hotel's boxed lunch that I had brought along. I inhaled the tuna sandwich, and then the potato chips, forcing the Crispy jingle out of my mind. I lay back and soaked up the sun.

A loud squawk brought me upright. It was the harsh call of a crow, but I couldn't see any sign of him. Made me wish Emerson were there, both to keep me company and retrieve the sticks I'd left in the car.

No bird, but on the other side of the field, a human. Too far away to determine the exact kind, but someone indeed was out there now. I didn't want to draw attention to myself, so I slunk behind a nearby outhouse, pulled out my Leica and zoomed in. Male. Tall. That's all I could tell because his back was to me. He was in sweat gear, exercising. Push-ups, jumping jacks, running in place, in rapid succession. A sight to behold. Arms, legs. Every limb in sync. His body at his command.

After several repetitions, he turned. I adjusted the lens, looked through the viewfinder again and felt a jolt. Could be. I fumbled through my wallet for the photo just to be sure. Compared the two. Light hair. Proud stature. High forehead. It *was* Joe.

I watched as he continued his routine, wondering why he would show himself so publicly, putting his body on display. Although perhaps that was the point, to telegraph that he had nothing to hide.

He was relentless, working out with the fervor of an Olympian. Joe was thirty-seven, Hiram said. Maybe he *had* been in the games. Could have even competed in '36, the year Jesse Owens shamed Hitler into silent fury. Or maybe he was just burning off some steam.

When he finished, he put a towel around his shoulders and stretched. Then he climbed the ladder. He fidgeted with the scoreboard, came back down. He collapsed the ladder and carried it to a small storage shed. Doing his job, it seemed. Maintenance.

Although an encounter was precisely what I'd been waiting for, I didn't know how to proceed. Approaching Joe there, with no one else around, would be too suspicious, especially because

I didn't have a believable enough script. So with him occupied, I limped back to my car, banking on the presence of an additional vehicle. And, indeed, there it was, parked on the other side of the lot. Then I waited, letting his actions dictate my next move.

After a half hour, I began to fear that he'd gone to perform another task or that he'd left another way, that the car wasn't his. But then he appeared. He had changed into street clothes, and before I could think, was starting his engine. I started mine, too, and followed him.

I've tailed a few people in my day, so I knew how to minimize my chances of getting caught. But this would be tricky, given we were the only two cars around. So I didn't leave immediately. I waited until he was almost out of the lot, turning right onto Freeport Boulevard (which, with Hollywood Boulevard as my comparison, was more like an alley) before I put my car into gear. Once I was close enough I memorized the rear of his maroon De Soto, the oblong window, the chipped paint near the bumper, and, of course, the plate number. After that, I kept my distance. He drove at a pretty good clip, but the roads were open enough that I had little trouble keeping up.

He was heading in the direction of his neighborhood, toward the American River, taking the route I'd driven the past several days. The same wide, flat expanse, the same thickets of marsh. I chewed on a stick, watching his head bob back and forth like a metronome. Must have been listening to music. Bach, I imagined, with the reliability of the beat. Or a Nazi marching song in his head.

I slowed, ready to take the exit toward his house. But Joe sped past the street, and a car ahead of me hampered my ability to follow. For a second Joe was out of view. Only a second. But, impossibly, the De Soto vanished. I was stunned, craning my neck around like a meerkat. There! I spotted the car making a U-turn. Where was he going? I raced to make the same turn. But the light at the intersection was red, with cars staggered at too regular an interval to take a chance.

"Fuck." I swore again and pounded on the steering wheel, too, for all the good it did me. Because even before the light had changed, I could see that I'd lost him.

# 18

## OBSTACLE INTERFERENCE

I decided to wait until after Christmas to resume my pursuit. Better to think and regroup. At least I'd seen Joe, verified his whereabouts. I'd seen the particulars of his car, too. And the intensity of his workout, likely a habit, hopefully at the same location.

In the meantime, I'd walk around town, treat myself to a couple holiday meals.

"Merry Christmas!" the doorman said.

"Same to you."

"Beautiful day."

I gazed up at the slate sky.

"Can I direct you anywhere?"

"Know a good spot for breakfast?"

He looked me over. "Waldo's. Other side of the park. Any path will get you there. It's a hole-in-the-wall, but they have the best omelets in town. Homemade bread, too. Always crowded, but only open until noon today, so better hurry."

I wondered what he would've recommended if I'd been a gringo, but the place sounded just to my liking. Waldo's. As in Ralph Waldo. Emerson's namesake. Champion of mind over matter. Individualism. Self-reliance. Principles I admired.

The apse was indeed gone and as the bellman had said, work on the new addition hadn't begun yet. But they'd appropriated portions of the park for lumber, sand, steel beams, and other construction materials. I stood in front of a crane, its boom lowered, decorated with a giant, red bow. An attempt to gussy up the disarray. Something that surely occurred inside the capitol as well.

Any path, the doorman said, so I chose the one with the fewest visitors, a narrow diagonal trail through a grove of trees, most of which were bare. A sign explained:

DEDICATED IN 1897. IMPORTED AS SAPLINGS FROM FAMOUS CIVIL WAR BATTELFILEDS. OAK, HICKORY, CEDAR, MAPLE, ELDER, DOGWOOD.

I shivered, felt a chill that no coat in the world could have prevented.

Trees. From the bloodiest of soils. Oak, Hickory, Cedar, Maple, Elder, Dogwood. Witnesses to heroes and cowards. They must have been beautiful in the summer, when their green leaves brought shade to the living. But today, their skeletons exposed the wounds, were reminders of the dead.

I opted for another path, the one with massive palm trees, incongruously dusted with frost. But if I'd hoped to escape the battle, I was sadly mistaken. Because here also were monuments and memorials, plaques commemorating Gettysburg, Antietam, Bull Run. I slowed, rubbed my leg. I knew the inscriptions without reading them, heard the cries of ghosts to whom they were dedicated. For a moment I sank into the 4-F abyss.

But this was Christmas, not my anniversary, and I wasn't

at the cemetery. I straightened and kept going, only pausing at a stand where a teenaged boy was roasting chestnuts. He seemed to enjoy it, smiling as he took orders. I focused on his nimble hands, turning and packaging the hot treats, releasing the pleasant aroma. Still, it was impossible not to see the life-size sculpture of a rifle-toting cowboy right beside him, gazing out with an enigmatic expression. I read the accompanying plaque:

TO THE VETERANS OF THE MEXICAN AMERICAN WAR.

Conqueror. That was the look. Written all over his lean, rugged face.

I approached the bronze figure, close enough to touch its icy surface. An impressive rendering. Boots, limbs, gun, all realistically portrayed. The musket had a long barrel, short stock. Looked ready to shoot. If I'd had the choice, which side would I have been on?

The traffic light was red. I waited, tapping my cane, like a blind man who'd dodged an invisible bullet. Green. I crossed, turned down 11th, breathing in the holiday, the momentary illusion of happiness.

I spotted Waldo's. Its windows were steamed up, but I could see the crowd within, not to mention the line out the door.

I could see something else, too. A final hurdle, it appeared, coming in the form of a clanging bell. And a cape, bonnet and military-style uniform. Of all things. A Salvationist, right in front of the restaurant, her skinny, socked ankles poking out from a calf-length skirt. I searched for an escape, left or right, even back through the battlefield. But then I stopped. The woman was stooped, her eyes crinkled from age. Not conniving. Not sensual.

Not anything like Penny's, as if that were something to fear. I could approach her without worry, without feeling manipulated. I dropped a fistful of coins into the bucket. They rang out like a winning slot machine.

"Bless you," she said. "God bless you, my son."

# 19

## CAMOUFLAGE

I'd slept through Christmas, waking up with what I thought was a cold. But ten days later, I was still flat on my back. The hotel staff did all they could, called the doctor, brought me toddies and soup, encouraged me to stay in my room. The flu, I was told. I called Hiram, who said they'd keep watch on the house for a few days. But it wasn't until the week after New Year's that I was back on the job, redoubling my efforts.

And those efforts paid off. I learned, for example, that Joe regularly maintained the football field, that it seemed to be his primary job. He planted and dug up things, moved around equipment, installed and changed lights. I also learned that he did indeed exercise out there, three times a week, later in the day with school back in session. I knew because I watched him. From the same bleachers as before, although I changed positions and limited my time. The presence of the students and faculty made observing more difficult, but it also provided cover. With the exception of my color, I blended in, dressing as a teacher, carrying books and an old briefcase I bought at a pawnshop. And I continued to follow Joe, to his car, and to that same, unpredictable turn.

The road where I'd lost him led to a bar, a dive called the

Flame that he frequented nearly every day. An unassuming building with a neon-flashing candle. Twelve creaky stools, a few scattered tables, dark, sticky wood. A little like Waldo's, only with booze on the menu.

For a week I just watched him go in. Then I went in myself, skipped two days to avoid notice, and returned. During that time, I saw nothing suspicious. Joe had no trace of an accent. He drank a couple beers, chatted with the bartender, a plethoric, hairless fellow named Carl, and a few other regulars. About football, the weather, his new baby boy, Roger, who'd been born on December 29th. And until now, he'd taken no notice of me. I needed a natural encounter, so I'd waited until an opportunity presented itself. Thursday, February 2nd, one finally occurred. The men had been talking about the war. About friends they knew who'd been killed, wounded. One guy told of a buddy who still had shrapnel in his belly. Another with a plate in his head. Everyone was telling stories. So I chimed in, pointing to my leg, for the first time in my life grateful for my condition.

"How'd it happen?" someone said.

"Broke it. Undercover mission in the army. I was tracking a Kraut and fell the wrong way. Not very heroic. At least the bastard was captured—by another soldier in my unit."

Joe sat stirring his drink, overtly unfazed by the insult. A few of the men whispered amongst themselves, perhaps doubting my account.

"At least you're alive," Joe said, still stirring.

I looked up. "Yeah."

"Where you from?" he said.

"L.A."

"Far from home."

"I'm here for work."

"Ah."

"You serve?" I asked.

"Navy."

Not only an American, but a vet. Good back-story.

Drinks kept flowing and the conversation turned domestic. The after-holiday letdown was palpable. All the men were grousing about bills, about wives who had spent too damn much on the kids. And the rotting garland that had yet to be removed from around the bar's mirrored wall only added to the gloom.

"Claire's a peach," Joe said, "but man, she spent a whole month's salary on the baby!"

"Be grateful you only have one." Carl said. "Try six!"

"Wives or children?" Joe said.

Everyone snickered in common cause. A reason for another round.

I took a swig of my beer. It was now or never, when everyone was loosened up. "That's capitalism for you."

They turned, as I'd hoped. I kept my eyes on my drink. "I mean the whole consumerism bit. You know, the American way, keep buying all the things you don't need."

For what felt like an hour, they were silent.

"Why don't you go somewhere else, then?" one of them finally said.

"Like where you came from, maybe," muttered another.

I straightened, looked them in the eye. "What's that supposed to mean?"

"Now, now," Joe said. "Man's an American. A vet. And he's got a point, doesn't he fellas? You all just said your kids have more toys than they'll ever use."

A couple of grunts, begrudging ones at that. Probably thinking I was too old and too brown to have fought. But Joe appeared to have taken my bait. Or maybe he was just curious, or suspicious. Whichever, he seemed to have some power over the others. They let it go and went to play pool. I ordered another beer.

"Name's Joe. Joseph Reynolds," Joe said, taking the stool next to me, as if he were in on my plan.

"Andrew Martin." I'd thought about giving a false name, but what if he looked me up? Instead I gave him my real false name, and then, to answer his obvious question, I said: "Changed it."

Joe's eyes were steel blue, implanted symmetrically under his sky-high forehead. His nose was straight, jaw square and lips so defined they seemed painted on.

"So what's your line?" he said.

"Law. Doing some temporary work up here. For the steelworkers union."

"You're a lawyer?"

"Shocking, huh? But yes."

"No, not shocking. I admire it. Wanted to be one myself. I'm a union man, too."

"Oh?"

"Yeah. NCDCL. Northern California District Council of Laborers, if you don't know.

"I do know."

"What are you doing for steel?"

"Actually, I'm not permitted..."

"Oh, of course."

"What do you do, Joe?" I said.

"Just a maintenance worker. At the college."

"Hey, don't diminish it. Labor is the backbone of the country."

Joe squinted at me. "You've been down to the Labor Market, of course. At the riverfront?"

I knew about the area, where migrants went to get jobs. Why would I go there? Why was he asking?

"Not yet," I said.

"Rough place."

I nodded. "By the way, thanks for standing up for me back there."

"Course. We vets gotta stick together, eh? None of those pricks fought."

I smirked.

"You married, Andrew?" he said.

"No."

"Too bad. I complain, but it's the only way to live as far as I'm concerned."

~

And that was it for a while. Another week passed. During that time I drove to the Labor Market. Parked and walked down 2nd. Just in case Joe had been testing me in some way. Rough wasn't the word. Made Skid Row look like Beverly Hills. Wall to wall employment agencies, if you could call them that. Broken glass, stench, trash everywhere. Men scrounging for food, sleeping in doorways. Looks of desperation. A paucity of cash and every other human need, including oxygen. The air was thick with smoke and soot from the nearby shipyards and factories, the only places that appeared to be hiring. Maybe it was better in the spring, when they needed field workers, when the migrants did the jobs they were trained for.

Now they hung out in the bars. Pool halls and bars. Hundreds of them. Men reeked of booze, yet were begging at corners. One approached me with an outstretched hand, the same color as mine. I felt a pang but kept walking, wondering if secret meetings were held behind any of those storefronts. If Joe had come here looking for Reds.

I'd gone to the Flame, too, but, except for a nod, Joe ignored me. I'd dropped the bait, thought he'd bitten. But maybe he hadn't liked the taste.

It was Monday, February 13th. Joe had just left and I was getting ready to settle up when I heard my name.

It was Joe. He'd come back in and was standing over me. "If you're alone, maybe you'd like to come over for dinner this week. Wife's a great cook."

Whatever the reason, Joe had taken his time with me. He was patient. I needed to respond in kind.

"Thanks for the offer," I said. "Can I let you know tomorrow?"

"Sure. But don't take too long. Claire is a perfectionist when it comes to entertaining. She needs a day or two to prepare."

"Understood."

"You won't be sorry," he said, as he pushed open the door. "And I might even have some suggestions for that leg."

20

## BEHIND ENEMY LINES

"Delicious," I said, and meant it. The duck, accompanied with asparagus and rice, was restaurant quality. I accepted another glass of wine and leaned back, stuffed but still starved for clues.

"Leave room for dessert," Claire said, clearing off the table.

Claire seemed as American as the apple pie she said was ready to come out of the oven. Wavy brown hair, hazel eyes, glowing complexion. Still plump, like a corn-fed farm girl. She claimed to be from Iowa. So did Joe. Born and raised there, both of Irish descent. It's where they met, they said. But when I asked if they had any photos, they said they were in storage, along with other personal belongings.

Hiram was ecstatic when I'd told him about the invitation. "*Mazel tov,*" he said. "This has to mean something. Whatever you're doing is working."

But I wasn't so sure. Over cocktails, it was I who steered the conversation to politics. I said that the unions were under attack, that all this Red scare business was a way to undermine them. I even said that although I was, of course, a loyal American, I thought Marx had a point.

Joe nodded, either in agreement or recognition that he'd

caught a fly. All he said was: "As long as I can provide for my family, I'm happy. I'm just glad we have the unions fighting for us."

Us. Meaning Claire and his baby. Roger was asleep, but he might as well have been the table centerpiece, because that's all Joe really wanted to talk about. How handsome his son was. How well-behaved. "And you should see the way he looks at me," he said. "Like he knows who I am."

Was he playing me? Maybe. But if he was acting, he was damn good at it. His adoration for his son felt real, although how would I know? Certainly not from personal experience.

"How long have you lived here?" I said.

"Just a year. We had an apartment in town before. But we wanted more space, with the baby coming. We want a large family. Of course, it would be hard to support one on my wages alone, but Claire has a small inheritance."

"Yes, I do," Claire said, kissing Joe on his head before placing the piping hot pie on the table.

"Lucky," I said.

The pie was extraordinary. So was Joe's account of his time in the navy. He told me the name of his ship, where it was stationed, the camaraderie of the crew. Stories of survival and death. Names of survivors, the brothers he mourned. He even showed me an official looking ID card, with a picture of him in uniform. Something that could be easily verified, but that, either way, would probably check out. Unlike me, which is why I told him I'd worked undercover. Just not for whom.

After dessert we relocated to the living room, decorated in a colonial style and including a Martha Washington desk and a half-filled bookcase. As we sat down, Roger started crying and the evening rapidly came to a close.

Not, however, before Joe demonstrated an excruciating stretch for my leg. Nor before I glimpsed a tiny, wire sculpture on a pedestal. No one else have would noticed. I wouldn't have if not for John. But I did notice, and could have sworn that it was made from a paperclip.

~

Who would create art from an office supply? A child perhaps. Or maybe someone for whom such a commonplace object had special meaning. Like holding together the pieces of his new identity, the documents that changed him from Nazi to neighbor. The governmental program. Operation Paperclip.

But why would he display such an obvious icon? Did he enjoy flirting with danger? Was it hubris? Maybe the same reason he exercised in public. To prove that there was nothing to it.

I had to get back in that house, so I intentionally left a glove in the bathroom. It was leather and expensive. One that would warrant a return trip, which I would make around eleven o'clock the next morning, when Joe was at work and Claire said the baby was usually awake. I would need a distraction.

~

I got up early, my muscles stiff and sore. Joe had increased feeling in my leg. I'll say that for him. Damn near pulled it out of the socket. When I asked how he'd become an expert in such matters, he said his father had been an athlete turned chiropractor, that he'd taught Joe about the importance of keeping in shape, admonishing him to treat his body as a temple.

The phone rang. It was only nine o'clock.

"Oh, Mr. Martin. Mr. Martin..."

"Martha?"

"Oh, oh...oh"

"Martha, what is it?"

"It's Emerson. Oh, dear, dear, dear..."

"Sick?"

"Worse. Oh, Mr. Martin, I'm so sorry. I don't know.... I went outside...for a second. You know how careful I am..."

"What is it, Martha!"

"He escaped, Mr. Martin. Flew the coop! Oh, oh. I'm so..."

I fell on the bed, broke out in a cold sweat. "Martha, are you sure? You've checked the cabinets, closets, yard?"

"Oh, you know I have. I've been frantic. Looking everywhere. Everywhere I tell you."

"Listen, Martha. Listen, please. I want you to do me a favor. I need you go to my apartment. See if he's there. It's locked up, but there's a cage outside on the patio. Check that. All the trees, too."

"But I can't leave..."

"Get that friend of yours to come over. Martha, I'm going to give you directions. You go there. You look everywhere, understand?"

"Yes, yes...all right."

"And call me as soon as you know anything."

I lay on the bed, every inch of me tense, as the hours ticked by. The thought of Emerson flying around L.A. on his own, lost perhaps, prey to human and beast, was unbearable. Finally around 3 p.m. the phone rang.

"Martha?"

"I'm so sorry," she said, sniffing. "No sign."

I held my hand over the receiver and sobbed.

"Mr. Martin? You know, I love Em."

"I know," I finally said. "It's all right, Martha. Just do me a favor and keep looking. Can you go back to my place tomorrow?"

"Of course. I'll do everything I can. I'll put an ad in the papers. In the Lost and Found."

"Thank you."

"His little girlfriend is depressed. I'm surprised he would leave her. I mean he seemed so happy here..."

"Probably an escape of opportunity. He is just a bird," I said, not at all believing my own words.

~

I took a Miltown and lay in bed the rest of the day. I considered going home. Maybe Emerson was holed up somewhere, waiting for my call. I envisioned myself roaming the city, spotting him on a branch, or a wire, or in Pershing Square. I might see him nestled in a shrub, or pecking at the pet store window. But if I couldn't find him, then where would I be?

It helped that I was on the verge of a breakthrough with Joe. If that little wire was what I thought it was. The following morning I took another pill. Shortly after eleven o'clock, I was knocking on the Reynolds' door.

Claire answered with a baby bottle in one hand and Roger in her other. She was in her robe and slippers, her hair in a tangled bun. "Oh, Andrew!"

"So sorry to bother you."

"No bother. I always like company. Come in."

"I think I left one of my gloves here. I would have called but I was near your neighborhood..."

"Yes, I have it. We didn't know how to reach you."

"I know."

"Well, sit down, sit down," she said. "Forgive how I look. It's been a rough morning."

"So that's little Roger."

"Not so little. He eats like a horse!"

I smiled.

"Want to hold him?"

Absolutely not. "Sure."

"Want some coffee?"

"Yes, thanks."

I had exactly zero experience with babies. I didn't know the first thing about how to hold one properly. Perhaps because I'd rarely been held myself. My mother. Did she ever cradle me? Cling to me? Adore me the way Claire, wife of a Nazi, did her son?

Roger squirmed, contorted his face. When he relaxed his muscles for a second, I tried to see a correspondence between his features and that of his parents. He did have a high forehead.

I was afraid to stand up holding him, so intentionally sat near the table upon which the curiosity was displayed. The wire. Painted white, twisted into an abstract shape. The pedestal was black. Tiny holes had been drilled into it to keep the object upright.

I was still studying it when Claire returned with the coffee.

"How are you two getting along?" she said.

"I'm not very good at this. He's cute, though. Has your eyes."

"Thank you," she said, whisking him up. She smirked. "What do you think of it?"

"What?"

"The *objet d'art*," she said in mocking French.

"Interesting."

"Oh come now. It's silly, isn't it? One day Joe and I went through the house and made things out of anything we could find. I made that one."

"Looks like maybe it was a paperclip?"

She giggled. "Yes, it was! I don't know if I should be flattered or insulted that you recognize it. And there's another masterpiece," she said, pointing to the desk. I won't be hurt if you know what *that* is.

I walked over to the desk and picked up the piece there. It was a shoe heel, painted beige with dark blue polka dots. I pretended to examine it, but was really looking at the desk's cubbyholes, stuffed with papers.

"And that frame on the wall there," Claire said. "Made out of a wastebasket."

"You're talented." And maybe cleverer than I thought.

"I won't make any money off them. I wish they had a union for housewives."

"I agree. Most important job in the world."

"No really. I think the government should take care of families. You know, provide health care, basic needs stuff. Share the wealth. Don't you, Andrew?"

"Yes, I do."

She winked. "You know, Joe and I really like you. Maybe we could fix you up with someone who thinks like we do."

"That's an idea. But, uh, I should be getting on my way," I said.

"Oh, do you have to? I've been sitting here wondering if I could ask a small favor."

"What's that?"

"I'd like to take a shower. It's been a couple days. Hope you can't tell! I'll be quick, and I'll put Roger in his playpen," she said. "I just hate leaving him unattended."

Too good to be true. "I suppose I could stay a little longer."

"You're a doll. Be right back," she said,

*Think like we do. Union for housewives. Government, families.* Was she fishing? The questions seemed almost too obvious. She might as well have asked: "Are you a communist?"

As soon as I heard the water running, I went back to the desk. Thumbed through everything, which turned out to be mostly bills. Plus a to-do list, measuring tape, other odds and ends that Claire might have turned into another project. I glanced over at Roger. The desktop was locked, but the key was in one of the drawers. The water was still on, so I opened it. More bills. Matches. Rubber bands. Nothing else. I locked it back up and headed to the bookshelf. Dictionary. Encyclopedia. Dickens. Austen. Several romance novels. *The Odyssey*. Quite the readers.

One section was devoted to Americans. Hawthorne. Hemingway. I ran my hands over the bindings. The books looked new. A thin volume, barely visible, was wedged in between Twain and Poe. A pamphlet of some sort. I slid it out. No title. I opened it, turned to the first page: *Turn Verein*. German! I stifled a gasp and stuffed it in my inside coat pocket.

The water had stopped. I heard some shuffling. The clomping of shoes. Whispering? Some other noise. Christ. I checked to make sure nothing was amiss, breathed to compose myself.

"Here you are," Claire said, handing me my glove.

She was in a different robe, towel drying her hair. Barefoot.

"Thanks," I said, trying to steady my trembling hand.

"Are you all right?"

"Yeah. Coffee must have given me the jitters. Had some earlier, too."

"I do make it strong."

"It was good. But now, I *do* need to go," I said.

She picked up Roger and showed me to the door. On the way out, I glanced again at the sculpture, which, from this angle, hinted at the shape of a swastika.

~

Any real spy would have immediately examined the goods. But the Miltown was wearing off, and with it my priorities. Before anything else, I had to call Martha again.

The sky was bright blue with puffy clouds. An advertiser's

dream. Such everyday beauty belonged to the world, but the space itself to birds. It was their birthright. Like Winkie and G.I. Joe, the famous World War II carrier pigeons. Birds that flew massive distances, saved hundreds of lives. They deserved a glance at heaven, if it existed.

But parrots weren't pigeons. Parrots were homebodies, attached to their earthly shelters.

I checked my rearview mirror. Traffic was mild. I checked again. Three or four cars staggered behind me. Behind those, another car kept pulling out as if to pass, only to pull back again. The color struck me. Maroon. A maroon sedan. I slowed a bit, letting the Plymouth behind me go by. The sedan slowed. I repeated the move, this time with a Ford. The sedan slowed again. Then, I pulled over to the shoulder and stopped. The sedan started to pull over, too, but changed course and kept on going. The car was a De Soto. And though the driver looked straight ahead, he couldn't hide his forehead. Or his license plate.

Joe. He must have been in the house. Or the garage, which had been closed. Claire's shower was probably a ruse, giving him the chance to move about. The clomping, the whispering. Maybe saw me steal the pamphlet. He was on to me. I went there needing a distraction, but was distracted myself.

I hightailed it back to the hotel, checking my mirrors the entire way. When I reached my room, I heard a commotion behind the door. I was alarmed, but it was only the maid. I gave her a buck and told her she could skip cleaning today.

I breathed and opened the pamphlet. *TURN VEREIN.* On the opposing page, an English translation:

*Gymnastics Club. Founded in 1854. 'Sound Mind, Sound Body. For German people and lovers of German culture.'*

The text surrounded a bold image of a discus thrower.

I got up and paced, my cane pock-marking the carpet. I pictured Joe on the field. Showing off his soundest of bodies. I thought you were Irish, Mr. Reynolds, I imagined myself saying. And yet, all of this, even him following me, was only circumstantial. Evidence, but not quite hard enough.

The next page of the pamphlet had a list of activities. Gymnastics, of course. Games. Picnics. Charity events. *Harmonie*, a musical celebration. Music, yes Germans like music. The next listed the members: Becker, Mayer, Fischer. Schmidt, Schneider, Weber. But no Reynolds. No Joe. No *Fraulein* Claire.

Martha! The operator put me through. The phone rang and rang. Probably sensed it was me. Finally, she answered. No. No Emerson.

I hung up with a stabbing emptiness and a fleeting image of Gringo, my father's cobalt macaw. I hardly ever thought of him, but it's where my affection for the creatures must have begun. Why Pop named him that I don't know because it would have been an insult. But he was handsome and smart and always cheerful. The day my father was arrested, however, marked the end of all that. Seeing his idol carted away in handcuffs unleashed a terrible fury, ending in him trying to bite the cop. After that, he became morose and never left his cage. He withered away, dying the day after my father was murdered. My grandmother and I mourned my father differently, but we gave Gringo a funeral fit for an eagle.

After an hour of misery, I called Hiram to convey the news. He wanted me to come over, pronto, said he'd have a cab waiting in the back entrance.

~

Hiram's wife, Pearl, answered the door. The name fit. She

was petite, with a round, pearl-like face. She must have been in her sixties, but was modernly styled. She wore a blue sweater that hugged her still youthful shape.

"Come, Mr. Martin," she said. "I was sorry I couldn't be here when you first arrived." She took my hand and led me downstairs. Her palm felt like a pearl, too, smooth and tiny.

Hiram was seated at a card table, munching on some grapes. He turned and motioned for me to join him.

"What can I get you, Mr. Martin?" Pearl said.

I told her I was fine, but she returned with pound cake and coffee.

"So, your cover is blown," Hiram said.

"Looks that way. Here," I said, feeling for the pamphlet. But where was it? I thought I'd... Goddammit. I'd had it when I was talking to Martha. The nightstand. "Sorry, Hiram. I was in quite a state. Must have left it at the hotel."

"Understandable. As long as you're sure it's there."

I nodded.

"You've done a good job, Andrew."

"Not good enough."

"Nabbing that wasn't easy, and it's a step."

"What happens now?" I said.

"We'll see."

"You know, Hiram, I've wondered. Why doesn't the government use our own spies? Seems as if everyone, except for Hollywood, and even a few of them, hates communists."

"Do you?" Hiram said.

I thought of my father and wanted to say yes. "Hate? No. But I'm a capitalist."

"I'd guess a lot of Americans feel that way. Hard to turn in one of your own. Nazis don't care whom they spy on. Soviets, Americans, it's all the same as long as it gets them off the hook."

"Maybe that's it."

"Tell me, Andrew. What's our friend like, I mean to talk to."

"Joe? Like anyone. You'd never know. That's the danger, isn't it?"

Pearl came back down and sat. "So, Mr. Martin," she said, touching my arm, "got a girl?"

"Pearl," Hiram said.

Pearl winked at me. "I'll bet your mother would like some grandchildren," she said.

"Pearl!"

"I'm just joking," she said. "I'm a notorious matchmaker. I fit the stereotype, as Hiram says." She smiled and patted my arm again. "And I wasn't thinking. Forgive me. Is your mother still with us?"

I thought for second longer than I should have. "No."

~

It was only eight o'clock, and I felt as if I were a speeding train whose brakes had been prematurely yanked. It was over. Just like that. Someone would come for the pamphlet tomorrow, and then I was done.

I needed a drink. I'd been meaning to try the Capitol Bar since I'd heard someone in the lobby rave about the generous pours. It was a block away. By nine, I was on my third round, listening to a congressman exchange a gin and tonic for a vote. The place was filled with sophisticates and political types. Normally, I would be humored. But I wasn't. I was agitated, still on the train tracks, still in gear.

The host brought me my coat and cane. He looked Indian, but his hand reminded of that beggar's in the Labor Market. I don't know why, but I got in my car and headed there.

Night had softened the edges of the area. It was seedy, the suffering obvious, but not quite as harsh. Despair in silhouette. The mercury had inched up. Hotel lights flashed on the drab pavement. Music bellowed out from bars and open windows.

A restaurant called Copa de Oro was open. It was spare for its name, but clean and crowded with laborers who must have just gotten paid. I ordered enchiladas and a tequila. There were too many lamps in the place, shining too brightly. The silhouettes turned into weary, overworked men. Many Mexican, some gringos. Except for the woman seated at a table next to me, dressed like an intellectual. Dark sweater and rolled up blue jeans. Loafers, with a penny in them. Her hair was braided. She was writing.

With booze in me, I felt loquacious. "You don't look like you belong in here," I said.

She ignored me, so I returned to my meal.

"I could say the same for you," she finally mumbled.

"I'll take that as a compliment."

"You shouldn't."

I chuckled. "Can I buy you a drink?"

"No thanks. I'm busy. And I'm not here to get picked up."

"Good. I'm not here to pick anyone up. Just looked like you could use some refreshment."

"No."

I ate and ordered another drink while she kept working. She wore thick glasses but was still attractive. After a while, she sighed and rubbed her neck. Then she called to a man at the table on her other side. "Paulo," she said, and motioned for him to join her.

He sat down. "You need to report this to the agency," she said. "The cannery isn't allowed to withhold your payment without due cause. And you being sick is not due cause. If they balk, you come back, and I'll put you in touch with someone who can help. ¿Comprendes?"

"*Sí*. I understand. *Gracias,*" the man said.

After he left I said: "Excuse me, I couldn't help but overhear. "Are you a lawyer?"

"God forbid. Social worker, if you must know."

"Ah."

"What's the 'ah' for?"

"I didn't mean anything by it. Just ah."

"Bleeding heart. Is that what you were thinking?"

"I wasn't thinking anything."

"Well, these companies take advantage first chance they can. I volunteer, find the right person for them."

"That's noble."

"Necessary," she said. "What do you do?"

"Well, I *am* a lawyer." I thought. "For labor."

She smirked. "Oh? Really? Do you know Manny Alvárez?"

"Uh, no. I'm here from L.A."

"Oh, then you must know Lisa Stein and Paul Masters and..."

I shook my head. "All right. I lied," I said, wondering if Joe had seen through me that easily, too. "I'm a lawyer. For the other side."

She smirked again. "I could tell. Your eyes are cunning. I don't see any empathy in them."

"That's cruel."

She removed her glasses and looked at me directly. "What are you here for, anyway? Work for one of the sharks?"

"No. I don't know why I'm here."

"Well, I've gotta go," she said. "Stick around. Maybe you'll figure it out."

I did. But I didn't.

~

I'd stuck around too long in fact, with nothing to show for it but the promise of a hangover for the ages. I closed my eyes, but then forced them back open. The hotel room was spinning. It needed to stop before I could let myself sleep. Otherwise, I'd spend the rest of the night over the bowl.

That broad was feisty, I'll say that for her. I admired her spunk, even if I disagreed with her politics. But did I disagree? What was so disagreeable? That she was trying to level the playing field? That she valued the laborer as much as the boss? That my father would have loved her? I didn't know. Maybe it was the tequila.

I flicked on the table lamp and thumbed through the pamphlet again. *TURN VEREIN*. Gymnastics. Music. Members. There was another page. Hadn't seen that before. On it were addresses, phone numbers. And there was something else. Not part of the pamphlet. A piece of notepaper, wedged in.

More names. Rick Morris, Corey Robertson. Michael Wilson. Not very German. Sounded more like a Yankee lineup. I twisted the lamp so I could see better. Rick, Corey, Wilson. Reed. Frank Reed. I shot up. Frank Reed? *The* Frank Reed? I read again. Frank Reed. That was no baseball player. I ran my hand over the soft, penciled script. No, that wasn't even a Dodger. That was evidence. Soft, but hard.

~

Frank Reed. Former senator, anti-Semite, House Un-American Activities Committee attack dog. A trifecta of qualifications. Poster boy for an operation like Paperclip. I could still see Frank's expression in my office that day. Way back at the beginning, when I asked him to confirm a rumor about Nazis being hired by the government to spy on Reds. His look had told me something. I just hadn't realized how much.

At two o'clock, the room stopped spinning and I fell asleep. I awoke at nine and called Hiram. "If Frank's involved," I said, "it's a done deal." There's no other reason Joe would have his name. Death camps Frank could live with. But he'd turn in his own mother if she made borscht for dinner."

Hiram stopped me. It was a hotel phone, but who knew who might be on the party line.

"Meet me in two hours on the Capitol steps," he said.

~

I unbuttoned my coat. It was warmer than it had been in weeks. The flags overhead were almost still. I stood to the side of the steps, leaning on my cane. Heels clicked around me, sounding like muted machine gun fire. An otherwise bare oak tree showed a tiny sprout.

In my hand was a box, which held the pamphlet. I had told the concierge I needed a container for a gift, so he asked me if I wanted some ribbon, too. "Red, white and blue," he said, the only kind we have." I accepted and tied a bow.

"Andrew," Hiram said, waving. He was walking toward me. In daylight, he looked older, more hunched than yesterday. But that gleam in his eye shone bright, reaching me before he did.

We both nodded.

"Here," I said.

"Patriotic," he said, with a wink. "I'm sorry we can't celebrate. Too risky to have you back at the house again. But we'll let you know what comes of this. The pamphlet is one thing. What you found in it might be worthy of a medal."

# 21

## D-DAY

I smoothed out the wrinkles of my coat, laid it over my skivvies and clicked the suitcase shut. The sound was pleasing, a rhetorical flourish signaling the end of the job that now felt complete. The group was satisfied. Frank Reed. How he'd weaseled his way into this scheme was a story waiting to be unraveled. Frank, working with Truman? I could picture Jake from the *Times* drooling if he ever got wind of it. Yes, I had come through. John said he was proud of me. Proud like a father, he'd said again.

And yet, there was a pit in my stomach, a nagging sensation that all was not well. If Emerson were home, I'd have been eager to get there. I'd have let him lick peanut butter off my finger, bought him a new preening toy. I'd have even moved his cage in my bedroom for a night. Maybe a week. But there had been no responses to the ads. No hints. No spottings. Martha had done all she could, but she had her menagerie to attend to.

It wasn't just that, though. It was what it meant to go back, south instead of north. Past instead of future. Old instead of new. Back to the same job, the same streets, the same goddamn leg. I dreaded it. A passing feeling perhaps. But in my mind's eye, L.A. seemed foreign, the courthouse a mausoleum, the walkway to my apartment studded with land mines. I had fought and won and yet the victory felt hollow.

I checked around the room, pulling back the flowered bedspread, opening and shutting the curtains, looking under the bed. I found a belt but it wasn't mine. Bathroom and closet all clear. I caught my image in the mirror. A few silver strands here and there, a crop of new wrinkles settling around my eyes. I hadn't noticed them before.

I hadn't noticed that small print hanging near the door, either. It was a black and white abstract of a woman. Just wisps of a pencil, but instantly knowable. A woman in motion. I must have passed it a hundred times.

The wind was rattling the hotel windows. I glanced at the print again. A dot for a breast, a circle for a mouth. The figure was saying something. What? "Call." "Call." That's what I thought anyway, what I almost thought I heard. "Call." Cici's command. Unadorned. Plaintive. I had planned to answer it when I returned, when I had Emerson to bolster me up. But now. Why wait, adding to the dread?

The number went through. I tapped my hand on the scratched glass overlaying the desk. My digits left marks, fingerprints that resembled the map of the coast route, the one I would take home. Longer than 99, but I wasn't about to return the way I'd come.

"Hello."

I froze, almost hung up. "Cici."

"Andrew. Finally."

Her voice was quiet and even.

"Sorry. I've been pretty busy," I said. "How...how is your cousin?"

"She's fine."

"That's good."

"She's always been fine."

"Oh?"

"Andy." She took in a deep breath and exhaled. "I'm pregnant. Six months along. It's yours. That last night, you know."

I made a sound, a grunt. Or a scream. I couldn't tell. Things were slowing down and speeding up. I was drowning or being smothered.

"Did you hear me?"

"Are you *sure* it's mine? How do you know?"

"Andy. You know that it's only been you."

I did know but didn't want to.

"I tried to get rid of it," she said. "But, uh, didn't work out. You don't have to worry, though. I'm putting the baby up for adoption. In fact, there's already an interested couple. But I need money. I can't ask John."

"Of course," I said.

"Send it to this address."

I somehow wrote: 148...some, some street. 60th? I couldn't feel the pen, the paper had liquefied.

"You got that?"

"Yeah. Cici. Are you all right?"

"I'll be fine. No one need know."

I think she hung up, but I couldn't be sure. I sat, staring at the flowered bedspread, the curtain, the carpeted floor, where only minutes before no trace of me remained. Now the room was imprinted, would never be free of me. Guts, heart and blood splattered on everything. A stain no maid could eliminate. People would sense it when they walked in. They'd shiver and asked to be moved.

~

After checking out of the hotel and wiring Cici more

money than she'd asked for, I drove seventy miles north from Sacramento, through vacant, windswept plains. I'd heard of the annual migration, of the unique habitat that drew dozens of species of fowl to the area. Until now, however, I'd had no desire to visit, feeling that doing so might somehow dilute my affection for Emerson. Peculiar, I know. Idiosyncratic, like the rest of me. But now the birds beckoned. Like Cici, they called out to me. Come to the refuge, they said, and do what needs to be done.

*The Sacramento National Wildlife Refuge was established in 1937 with funds from the Emergency Conservation Fund Act of 1933 to provide refuge and breeding habitat for migratory birds and other wildlife, provide habitat and manage endangered, threatened, or sensitive species and alleviate crop depredation.*

So read the brochure I'd picked up at the visitor's center. "*Peak time to watch: November through February.*" It was Wednesday, February 22nd, three o'clock in the afternoon.

*In 1937, the federal government purchased the 10,775 acre Spalding Ranch and christened it the Sacramento Migratory Waterfowl Refuge. From 1937–1942 the Civilian Conservation Corp's 'Camp Sacramento,' housed up to 200 men at the current headquarters area. The men constructed levees, water control structures, and delivery ditches to create and sustain wetlands across the majority of the refuge.*

I had driven around the horseshoe shaped marsh on one of the dirt levees those men had built. Now, I leaned back on a bench, tilting my face toward the orange sky. The air was frigid, but the wind had calmed. I took two Miltowns from my pants pocket and swallowed them down with what was left of my rum.

I imagined those men who shaped this land, mosquito bitten, dust-choked. Scorched, thirsty, hungry. Like my brothers in the fields. Real and dreamed.

~

*"Mijo, see these men. See how they work? They're your kin. Hermanos. Don't ever forget it."*

*"I won't, Pop."*

*"Whatever I do, I do for them. And for you."*

*"I know."*

~

*Waterfowl migrate to the Sacramento Valley by the millions from as far away as Alaska, Canada, and Siberia. Sacramento Valley habitat supports approximately 44 percent of wintering waterfowl using the Pacific Flyway, attracting more than 1.5 million ducks and 750,000 geese to its seasonal marshes.*

I leaned back farther, my head parallel with the sky. Black, winged silhouettes appeared here and there. Then, there and there and there. Increasing exponentially, dividing and multiplying. Sublime and monstrous. Mother birds, father birds, baby birds.

Now I remembered. Bullock's. The department store window. What that family, the kid with the weird look, reminded me of. It was me. *My* family. Right before my mother supposedly died. When we all went trick-or-treating. Pop was angry.

~

*"What's wrong, Pop?"*
*"Nothing, Mijo."*
*"But, Pop..."*
*"Some things are best unsaid."*
*"But..."*
*"Enough!"*

~

Squawks and cackles. What *things*? Loud. Louder. Thousands of them squawking and cackling. I held my ears.

*Do not approach wildlife; instead use binoculars to view them from a distance, and remain quiet.*

I didn't need binoculars. I could envision every beak, every crest and plume. Mallards and geese, bufflehead and hovelers. Screeching out a concerto. A love song. A requiem.

*Hunting, which largely pays for the refuge, is permitted outside the range of the driving tour on Wednesdays and weekends.*

It was Wednesday, anyway. And there were no other cars around. I swallowed another pill. I wasn't floating. And I wanted to float. Float, and then fly. Migrate. Blend in with the scenery. Disappear. My leg alone wouldn't do. All that hunting. For what?

I had the gun with me.

I put the barrel to my head, thinking of destiny again. James. 4-F. John. Cici. And the café stop, the casual, fateful purchase. Everything had led to this. Meant to be. I pulled back the hammer, no longer belonging to myself. Tears streamed down the face that used to be mine. Pull. Pull!

Coward. I was a fucking coward, and now I wasn't alone. Someone else was here. Worse, he was heading my way. I covered the gun in the newspaper in which I'd brought it.

"Hey, d'ya see that that! Over there! Swooped right by you. Rough-legged hawk!"

The man bobbed all around, peering through his giant binoculars. "Where'd you go to you little beauty?"

I was dizzy, shaking.

"You missed it!"

A couple of cameras hung from the man's long neck. He had a long face, too. Long legs, long hands. Long nose that stuck out from his army green hat. He wore a backpack and hiking boots. "If I can get a photo, the club will be dazzled." He kept peering. "Bird-watching club."

I leaned back on the bench, catching my breath.

"Shoot," he said, after a few minutes.

I looked up. "Huh?"

"Must have found her prey." He sighed and let the binoculars sway. "Join you?"

He sat on the bench, not waiting for an answer. "Coffee?" he said, pulling out a thermos from his duffle bag. He didn't wait for an answer then either, but I took the offered cup.

"Walter," he said.

"Andrew."

He looked at me, really for the first time. "You all right?"

I managed a yes.

He spotted the empty bottle. "On a trip?" he said.

"Yeah."

"Know anything about birds?"

"Not much."

"Well, that one that flew by you is rare around here. *Chordata* phylum. *Accipitridae* family. *Buteo* genus. Feathered all the way down to her feet. Rough-legged, you know. I heard her call and followed. Sounds like a harpie." Walter wiped his runny nose and looked at me again. "You sure you're all right?"

I sipped, fighting back tears.

The birds thinned out, leaving the sky to paint itself a fiery gold.

"Everything looks better with coffee, eh? You drink that down." He got up and gave the binoculars another try.

Please go, I thought. Please. I traced the outline of the gun.

"Come here! Come here!" Walter was motioning to me frantically. "Come, come, come! Look!"

I put down the cup, made sure the gun was covered, and forced myself up. He handed me the binoculars.

"Right over there, hovering. See! See those delicate wings. The pale head. Black belly patch. Female. I was right. Now don't you go anywhere baby," he said, raising his camera. Click. Click. "That's a girl." Click.

I was standing, doing what he asked, despite the fact that I was finally beginning to float. The lens was powerful. Night was encroaching, but I could see the bird's pattern. It was bold. Dark and white. The pale head. She *was* hovering. Must have had dinner in sight. I thought she would dive any minute. But she didn't, as if she knew we were watching. Putting on a show."

"There she goes," Walter said, as she finally soared off.

I gave him back the binoculars and sat down on the bench.

"Another cup?" he said.

I shook my head.

"Well. I gotta be heading back. Family's waiting for me. Wife's making my favorite meal." He looked at me, harder this time, and slapped my shoulder. "Remember, no huntin' here."

"Yeah."

He gathered his gear.

It was nearly dark. Courage, I said to myself. Walter had reminded me of the world, that there were good people in it. If I believed in miracles, I'd say he'd saved me. But I didn't. If anything, he'd made me more determined, showing me the kind of man I'd never been, could never be. Friends. Wife. Children. God help me, children. I *was* a coward. Hated to suffer, afraid to love.

I felt for the gun again. But then I saw the newspaper, opened to the back page: PARADE PLANNED. I could just make out that scrunched up headline. The kind of news people liked. And that one, too. Something about needlecraft. I cocked my head to make sure I saw it right.

And then I blinked. Blinked again. Leaned in. I picked up the whole package, brought the paper close.

BUYERS LIKE FAIRHAVEN NEEDLECRAFT.

Fairhaven. I read on.

*The dainty items of needlecraft were being purchased rapidly as the second day of the sale got under way this morning. Delicate baby clothes including caps, sweaters, panties and bibs all hand crocheted from soft, fluffy yarns and in the three traditional colors, white, pink and blue were among the popular items purchased.*

Had to be.

*The bulk of the needlework being sold was made by the unwed mothers who have received shelter and medical care at the Fairhaven Home during the past year.*

Fairhaven. Penny. Pleading with me. *Your mother is alive.* My mother. And now. What were the chances? The odds of the thing. Was I dreaming again? Was I already dead?

~

Maybe it was another form of cowardice. Turning a kindly birdwatcher, a bit of journalistic drivel, into divine intervention. Had I always been a fake, a phony nihilist looking for an easy way out? All I knew was that I was back in my car, slowly emerging from the intoxication I'd hoped would have softened the lethal blow. I felt utterly detached, yet ached down to my cells. I was without faith, yet following signs. I was a man who wasn't there, with my hands on the wheel.

I took the Stockton turnoff. The first person I asked, a gas station attendant, gave me directions. "Drive down Main," he said, way past the university. Keep going. You'll think you're in the middle of nowhere. Turn left, left again, around the big open field. Then you'll see it on your right. Across from the church. Looks like a giant army barracks. They made it intentionally hard to find."

Beyond the university, there were no street lamps so I turned on my high beams. Desolate. Soon I spotted the field. Puny and empty. Then the church. Ditto. And there it was. Barracks, indeed. A few outside lights shone on the elongated, two-story building. It appeared grey and ironically barren, devoid of any ornamentation.

I turned into the parking lot. A tall, wrought iron gate, with a plaque reading FAIRHAVEN HOME FOR GIRLS was open, so I drove in and parked. I turned off the engine and leaned back.

Stars twinkled through the steamed up windshield. I could see my breath. I gazed at the light coming from the Home's twenty or so windows. The Home. My home. I thought of it now. Not my apartment, with the terrible void, but Boyle Heights, where my mother once lived. Where she left me behind. Where her love might have saved me. There were windows there, too, but no air, no light. See-through curtains that might as well have been opaque.

A few of the Home's windows were open. Which room was which? Were there babies in there? I felt like a baby myself, not knowing if my legs would carry me to the door. As if I hadn't yet learned to walk. They both felt flimsy, the left as much as the right.

A bell clanged. Again, I considered the possibility that I was already dead, the sound tolling for me. Through one of those windows I could see movement. Human shapes scurrying.

I searched in vain for my cane. Front seat, back. I'd only brought one, and now it was gone. Had I left it at the refuge? I exhaled and pushed open the car door. I stood. My legs buckled as soon they touched ground, feeling as if they'd sunk into quicksand. But I knew it was only dirt, so I willed myself up, mind over matter, and limped through the imaginary muck. Down a walkway, up two steps, to a double door. There was no bell. No knocker. Only a speaker, with a button.

I pressed it and waited.

"Yes?" said a female voice.

I opened my mouth but couldn't speak, as if I hadn't yet learned that skill either.

"Hello?"

"I'm here to see Penny," I finally said.

"And who are you? Penny doesn't have appointments at this hour."

"My name is Andrew Martin. Andrew Martin, a lawyer, from L.A."

No response. Silence for a minute or more. Then a commotion, steps. A porch light switched on, the door opened halfway. "Hello," said a young redhead. She was in a white uniform. Freckled and chubby, with compassionate eyes. "Mr. Andrew Martin. From Los Angeles, you say?"

"Yes."

"I'm sorry, but I'll need some identification."

I handed her my driver's license and business card. She examined them, and me. Then she smiled, and I thought, welled up a little. "Please," she said. "Come in."

~

She led me down a short hall into an office and closed the door. "Please, sit."

I obeyed. I looked around the room but couldn't focus.

"Penny is gone for the night, Mr. Martin. But I know she'll want to see you. I'm Rachel. I trained with her. We're friends. Close friends."

"Oh..." I was disappointed to the point of despair.

"You'll stay here, tonight," she said. "You look like you could use some sleep."

"Oh no. I can't."

"Mr. Martin," she said. "Please. You must."

An admonition. A command. Like Cici's.

"We have a room for guests, family members. It's vacant now."

"All right. I, I appreciate it. But, Miss...Rachel. Maybe you know... my mother... "

She nodded. "Yes, I know."

"Is she still here? Is my mother..."

"I know you must be anxious, but I'm not permitted," she said. "Penny will tell you. She'll be back tomorrow."

# 22

## IN THE TRENCHES

I awoke to a loud clang. The breakfast bell, I learned, the same one that had rung for dinner the previous night. My stomach was growling, but my mind was once again tortured, flooded with uncertainty. John. Cici. My mother. *Penny will tell you.*

Still, I had slept, deeply and dreamless except for a moment when I'd felt the presence of someone. Or something. Like a vibration or a chord, fleetingly tugging at me. I'd bolted up, but saw only my reflection in the mirrored table lamp beside the bed.

The visitor's room was in an alcove off the basement, and I hardly remembered walking there, let alone getting my suitcase, but I must have because here I was, in a yellow painted cubicle with a crucifix on the wall and my clothes in a heap on the adjoining bathroom floor.

There was a knock on the door. Rachel was standing just outside.

"Good morning," she said. "Sleep well?"

I nodded.

She had a tray with pancakes, bacon and coffee.

"Here you go," she said. It's not gourmet, but it's filling. I imagine you'll want to use the shower. Do you have clean clothes?" she said, eyeing the heap.

"No."

"Give them to me."

"Not necessary."

"I'll be back for you at ten. With the clothes."

Rachel obviously saw my confusion. "Be patient. I tried calling Penny to see if she could return earlier. Unfortunately, I couldn't reach her. But I promise, she'll be here this evening. In the meantime, a tour."

"I'm really not up for any tour. I have a bum leg."

"We have plenty of wheelchairs," she said, implying once again that I had no choice.

What did Rachel know that only Penny could tell me? The answer was obvious. I knew it the minute I'd arrived, even before perhaps. My mother had died. Really died this time. She'd been ill. I was too late. But too late for what? A phrase out of some movie. I didn't feel anything. I wasn't even sure why I was here, if it was my mother I'd come to see.

In truth, of course, I had a choice. I could have just upped and left. But I didn't.

~

The wheelchair solved the immediate issue of my leg and warded off other potential problems. Odd, but I wasn't ashamed. After yesterday, how could I be? There was a kind of peace in giving myself over, in not fighting. And no one was here to stop me. Not my mother, I knew that now. Not my father. No one to harden me against myself.

*"Get up, Mijo."*

*"I just want to lay here."*

*"Be a man!"*

*"James is dead! Have you forgotten? I'm mourning him."*

*"I know you're sad. But you're the son of warriors. Your grandfather died in battle. Do you know how many friends he lost? And yet he fought."*

*"I'm not a warrior. At least not for your cause."*

*"What kind of son are you, then?"*

*"I'm nothing. I'm a son of nothingness."*

~

With the exception of the guest room, the basement was dark and damp. The cement smelled moldy.

"Here's where they wash the diapers," Rachel said, rolling me past a steamy room with vats of boiling water. Inside, two girls with protruding abdomens looked at me with blank expressions. Their child faces were wet from the steam.

"This is Mr. Martin. A visitor from L.A.," Rachel said.

I nodded as they went back to their work.

"Diapers?" I said to Rachel.

"Oh yes. The girls deliver at the hospital in town, and then return here with their babies until they're adopted. Or the mother decides to keep them.

"Does that happen often?"

"Not often, but sometimes. Once they've bonded, it's a little harder to give them up."

*I tried to do away with it. Didn't work out.*

What did Cici mean, didn't work out? Couldn't get a doctor? Botched job? Had she suffered?

Rachel whizzed me into an elevator that opened to the lobby. I'd passed through before, but in the light of day it looked depressing, spare and sterile. Down the hall, the scene was out of Dickens. Girls were at work there too, sweeping and mopping.

"Those are the dorms," Rachel said, pointing. You're not allowed, of course, but there are six girls to a room. One shared bathroom at the end of the hall."

Next was the kitchen, where pork and beans were being prepared by uniformed Salvationists with aprons. Again, there were girls doing chores, washing and drying, cleaning out cabinets. They regarded me warily, as if I were an inspector or perhaps the father—or grandfather—of their unborn child.

The final stop, however, was a bright and sunny space, with light streaming through a large, bay window. There were cozy chairs and sofas. A fire was burning in a small stone hearth. The girls there, four in all, also appeared more content than the others, no doubt because they weren't engaged in hard labor, which would come soon enough. Instead they were crocheting, turning shapeless pastel yarn into art and warmth.

*Buyers Like Fairhaven Needlecraft.* This must have been where the goods publicized in the paper had been produced.

"Morning, ladies," Rachel said.

They responded with the soft clicking of needles.

"This is Mr. Martin. He's an attorney and is doing some work for us."

All eyes were on me—and the wheelchair.

"He's injured his leg," Rachel said.

There was something so soothing in the scene. It felt like a comfortable living room, a place to unburden one's troubles. Or at least to relax with them for a while.

"All the girls learn to crochet and knit at Fairhaven. It's their only real outlet," Rachel said. "It's all the director thinks they..." She blushed. Her freckles turned scarlet.

"Pardon?"

"Nothing. I don't know what I was going to say."

"Rachel! I've been looking for you. You're needed in the infant wing. STAT!" The order came from a hefty woman in hospital garb.

"Mr. Martin, stay here, please. I'll be back as soon as possible."

Before I could say I'd return to my room, Rachel was gone. I wheeled myself over to the window as if something had caught my attention outside. A plot of dead grass and the parking lot is what I saw, but I looked out intently, pondering Rachel's remark. It's all the director thinks they...what? Deserve? Are capable of?

"What happened to you?"

I turned. It was one of the girls, sitting Indian style on a high back chair, wearing slacks and a maternity blouse. Not much of a tummy from what I could see. I thought for a moment. Different audience, different cause. "Hurt myself playing basketball," I said, and rolled a little closer.

"My name is Lucy."

"That's nice work," I said, pointing to whatever she was making.

"Thanks. Who are you here to see?" she said.

"I can't discuss that."

"She cocked her head at me. "Are you Mexican?"

"Mexican American," I said.

"Martin isn't a Mexican name."

Nosy little thing. Couldn't have been more than sixteen. "I changed it."

"Ah. You know, Rachel's liable to be a while. There's always some emergency with the babies. Or with the nine-monthers. I'm only six months along."

My stomach somersaulted. *I'm six months. It's yours.*

"Shush," another girl said. She shook her head, indicating she either desired quiet or didn't approve of the conversation.

Lucy rose from the couch. "Let's go over there," she said, wheeling me to a love seat away from the others.

"I'm not an invalid," I said.

"Sorry. Should have asked." She sat down and crossed her legs again. "What to know how I wound up here?"

I must have gasped, because she snickered. She put down her needles and leaned forward. Her eyes were dull brown, but determined.

"A boy forced himself on me," she said. "I tried to stop him, but I couldn't."

Her tone was flat, matter-of-fact. She didn't whisper or tremble. I'd heard the line before, but not with such lack of emotion.

"Don't believe me, do you?"

"Why shouldn't I?"

"My parents didn't believe me either. They don't even come to see me."

I was silent. I hoped she was wrong about Rachel taking a while.

"I'm fine though," she said. "My baby will be adopted by a good family."

"You don't want to keep it?"

"Keep it? I'm not ready to be a parent. I didn't choose to be. You know what I'm gonna do after I get out of here?" she said.

"What?"

"Help other girls in my predicament."

"That's good," I said.

"There are so many poor souls in this place. I can take care of myself, but some of the girls. They need help. A lawyer," she said pointedly. "A friend. Want to hear more?"

"Should you be telling me?"

"They're just stories. No names. We're all given different names when we arrive. Like you, Mr. Martin."

I shifted in the chair.

"For privacy. And so we don't humiliate our families any more.

The lawyer in me sent up a warning flag. If I were in L.A., I'd close my ears, advise against giving me unsolicited information. But I wasn't in L.A. And she wasn't asking for legal advice. I watched as she crocheted, one loop after another.

"All right," I said. "Go ahead."

So she did. Told me about the girl whose boyfriend had died in a car accident right after asking her to marry him. And the one who'd nearly killed herself trying to perform an abortion with a hanger. There was the girl who'd never dated and went "all the way" one night because she thought it might be her only chance. The girl who liked girls but tried to prove to herself that she didn't. And the Jewish girl, as Lucy called her, a reference that shot through me like the bullet that almost had.

"Did you know we have to repent here, Mr. Martin?" she said. "There's a minister who comes to visit. Makes us kneel and beg for forgiveness. Even the Jewish girl had to do that, kneel before a cross. So her shame, the shame they make all of us feel, was doubled. She had the baby a month ago. A nine-pound boy. Nearly killed her. She got sick with hives, sick with disgrace. Still, as usual, they made her bond with her son. Bond with him before surrendering him in the care of another. Do you think that's fair?"

Perhaps Lucy had cast a spell with her stories. Perhaps it was Cici. Perhaps it was the wheelchair, the weakened condition it symbolized. But something rigid inside of me softened at hearing the plights of these girls, even though the sensation—empathy, I supposed—felt dangerous.

Lucy checked the clock and abruptly rose. "Oh, sorry, nearly forgot! I'm on kitchen duty. Nice meeting you, Mr. Martin."

"Likewise," I said and wheeled myself back to the window.

A few minutes later Rachel reappeared. "Finally!" she said. "Just a bad case of colic. The wailing can seem foreboding to the uninitiated. Ready to go back to your room?"

"Yes."

"Have a good talk with Lucy?"

I started to nod, but then wondered: how did she know?

~

At six o'clock Rachel informed me that Penny had arrived and would call for me at eight. She'd wanted to come immediately, but one of the girls' parents had unexpectedly demanded a meeting. I'd spent the remainder of the afternoon in bed, letting the day, and the days before, wash over me, drifting in and out of sleep. I'd heard the dinner bell at what I thought was only a few minutes earlier, so I was surprised to learn that it was now nine. Had I missed Penny?

I shaved, dressed and waited. My hands were sweating. A few minutes passed. I drifted again, dreaming of man-eating birds and half-formed babies, of guns and swastikas. I shook myself awake. Perhaps I'd misheard. But then....

"Mr. Martin?"

I recognized the voice, inhaled the jumbled scent penetrating the closed door. I wiped my hands on my pants and twisted the knob.

"Hello," Penny said. "Sorry for the delay. I'm so very glad to see you."

I almost didn't recognize her. She was in street clothes, trousers and a grey pullover sweater with a pink scarf tied around her neck. Her hair was curled, half up, half down, about like I felt. Silver earrings dangled from her small but slightly protruding ears. "Really? I thought I might not be welcome," I said.

"Why?"

"Just showing up like this. I mean, after what I said."

"I was surprised, of course. But very glad." She smiled, but not in a cheerful way. "I hear you spent some time in the sewing room."

I nodded.

"Let's go there to talk. We'll have it to ourselves. Here, I'll push you," she said, hand on the wheelchair that was still in the hall.

She'd obviously been debriefed—about everything. "I don't think I'll need that," I said.

"Actually, Mr. Martin, I think you might."

# 23

## LAND MINE

A fire was burning again in the hearth. The sight calmed me a little, although Penny's warning clanged in my ears as loud as the dinner bell.

Penny switched on a lamp. She positioned me near the fire, pulled up a chair and lit a cigarette.

"You don't look like a Salvationist right now," I said.

"I hope that's a compliment."

It was.

"Like one?" she said, offering a Lucky Strike.

I didn't have sticks with me. Would it have mattered if I had? "Yes," I said, accepting both the smoke and a light.

"So, you want to know about Isabella? About your mother?"

"I already do. She died, didn't she?"

Penny walked to the window and stood with her back toward me. "Yes."

"When?"

"A month ago."

I thought I might cry. Why, I didn't know. Some imitation of sadness. Or obligation. Instead I rose from the wheelchair, as if pushed from underneath. I steadied myself, limped over to Penny and embraced her. It was spontaneous. A novelty for me. Penny held me for a moment, then pulled back. "Mr. Martin."

"Andrew," I said.

"Andrew. Let's sit down."

We did.

"To simply say she died doesn't do your mother justice. There's much you don't know about her. Much you should know. Isn't that why you're here?"

I inhaled, held on to the smoke until I had to breathe. "I'm not sure."

"Something did change in you, though. You didn't even believe me when I came to L.A."

"I didn't want to."

"So what happened?" she said.

What happened? I'd heard that question before. From doctors and therapists. From bartenders and priests. Women had asked me, too. Hoping to get to my essence. Usually, I'd skirted the answer. There was always a gap between us, like the screen in a confessional. But Penny was different. I'd fought it, but from the very first moment, I felt that screen start to drop. Call it what you will, chemistry, energy, soul. Or that chord I'd sensed. All I knew was that her scent permeated my skin that day and never really left. Maybe that's why I'd come. To finally respond. To speak person to person. So I told her. About 4-F. About my leg. Even about Cici. Even about the refuge.

Penny took it all in quietly, only nodding now and then.

"I'm so sorry," she said. "You've suffered. Deeply. And I'm sure the woman you describe, Cici, has suffered, too. Is still suffering no doubt."

I exhaled whatever was left in me. "We all suffer."

Penny rose again, lit another cigarette. "Of course, I'm surrounded by mothers here. New mothers. Almost mothers,

mothers in waiting." She leaned on the wall, for support it seemed. "I was once one of them."

"Oh?" Another somersault.

"Yes. So you see I understand how these things can happen. And my own mother nearly disowned me for it. She was a Salvationist, too. Of the most ardent kind. Morally unyielding."

As I had been. As I still was perhaps.

"I had the baby here ten years ago. A boy, adopted two weeks later," she said, her voice trailing off.

All right. So she'd had a baby out of wedlock. It seemed as if everyone had, or would. But there was more. I could sense it. This was only a prelude.

"I've been working here ever since," she said. "It's why I joined up. Don't get me wrong. The organization does some good work. But their emphasis on discipline is misplaced. I stay because the girls need someone on the inside, someone who understands. There are a few of us trying to reform things, work within the system. Rachel is one of them. And Lucy has taken up the mantle, as well, become a kind of protégé."

That's how Rachel knew Lucy had talked with me, I thought. They must have planned it.

"For a few years, I worked elsewhere, too," she said. "In a mental institution. For women."

"That's something I know a little about. The institution part, anyway."

"Then Andrew you must know, too." She licked her lips. "You must know about the sterilizations that have occurred in those places. The eugenics influence."

"Yes," I said.

"And you must know that many of the victims are of Mexican descent."

Goethe. "Getty." Yes, I knew that, too. Obviously, I thought it a monstrous practice. Prosecuting my people was one thing. Cutting them open, removing their tubes and glands for the sake of racial purity, quite another. Or was it? At that moment I wasn't sure. Was it so different? I could have been their first line of defense. I'd had my reasons. But hadn't I contributed to the injury, used the law to justify my own kind of cut?

Something clattered outside. We both jumped, but Penny kept talking.

"That's where I met your mother."

I suddenly thought of the Sphinx. Head of a woman, body of lion, wings of a bird.

"She was older, hospitalized for depression. She'd been in prison. For prostitution." Penny sighed. "I remember that day well."

I signaled for her to continue, dreading but needing to hear whatever was to come. She may have looked inscrutable, but Penny was no Sphinx. She was a link, a conduit, a tunnel to my origins.

She flicked off some ash and sat back. "I'd spent the morning following a psychiatrist around, meeting the patients who were well enough to go on walks. That's the kind of thing I'd been hired for. Walks, letter writing, listener. I had no formal training, but I'd learned a lot about mental illness from years working at the Salvation Army. The down and out are often that way because of it." She smirked. "And I learned from my father. My mother was so rigid, so unforgiving, she drove him mad. Well," she said, "to drink anyway."

I smiled at the lighthearted way she'd characterized what must have been a painful memory. She had a sense of humor.

"I had met several young girls that morning, none over twenty years old. And I'd just seen the movie *Snake Pit*, with Olivia de Havilland. So I was primed. Ready for horror. And the place wasn't far off from the portrayal. Bars on the windows, torment around every corner."

Penny took a deep drag on her cigarette, as if doing so would block out the images in her head.

"A few of the girls were unreachable, too ill for my offerings. But others wanted to talk, tell me what brought them there. Nearly all of them were victims, their disease caused or exacerbated by neglect or abuse. One sunken-eyed patient whispered to me that she heard voices because of the poison her husband had put in her milk. The doctor, a brilliant clinician and decent enough fellow, dismissed the claim as paranoia, a classic symptom of psychosis. But I wondered. Had he checked her blood for metals? Had the husband had her committed? Can any man really understand what women suffer?"

Penny stared at me, as if the last question were more than rhetorical. But I didn't have an answer.

"Anyway," she said, "it had been a difficult morning. Even for someone like me, who had seen people at their worst, it was hard not to despair."

Penny stood up and threw her cigarette into the dwindling fire. I hoped that she couldn't go on, that I had dodged another bullet. But she sat back down.

"In the afternoon, the doctor took me to the wing for the elderly. Equally dismal but quieter. We entered a stark room with eight beds. 'This is Isabella,' the doctor said, flipping through the pages of her medical chart. 'Been on the streets,' he whispered. He nudged me to read. *Sterilization*. 'She's had a pretty rough time.' "

"There were five other women in the room. One was reading, another singing to herself, the rest sleeping. Your mother was lying on her side, her face away from me. Her legs were like flexible toothpicks, twisted and poking out of a flimsy blanket. Her white hair was in a bun. She turned at the doctor's voice. Her face was weathered, drawn, lifeless.

"'Isabella, this is Penny,' the doctor said. 'She's going to sit with you a while. Is that all right?'"

"Your mother gazed at me. I was surprised how directly, how light suddenly flickered in her eyes. I can't explain it, but I felt an instant connection to her. For the young girls earlier I'd felt sorrow and compassion. For your mother I also felt warmth. Maybe it was her age, maybe her softness, a vulnerability I'd never seen in my own mother. Whichever, the feeling appeared to be mutual. She asked the doctor to leave and took my hand."

Penny touched my own hand, which felt glued to my lap. "She'd made a mistake, Andrew, like many of the girls in here. Like me. And she paid for it dearly. But despite her anguish, she was kind. And lovely. She must have been beautiful when she was young. You have her smile, you know."

I was silent. A mix of emotions that I couldn't identify let alone articulate. But one word finally did slip out: "Sterilized." I could see the knife, slicing into my mother's brown skin, removing what they considered to be tainted flesh.

"Yes. A victim of the most heinous sort."

A wave of nausea nearly overtook me. I breathed rapidly until it passed.

"Your mother had nowhere to go, wasn't a threat to anyone. I grew close to her and convinced the director to let her stay here."

"That was good of you."

"We were friends. More than that. Before she came here, we wrote to each other. For her, it was catharsis, a way to..." Penny's eyes widened. "Wait. Stay put."

The second time in a day I'd been left in the sewing room. Not a coincidence perhaps. I felt in need of some stitching up.

I limped to the same window where I had earlier stood. A

bright half-moon shone in the darkness, its other half in muted outline. I was numb and on edge, closed and open. Hungry for more but overly full. A study in opposites.

"Andrew," Penny said. She had returned and was motioning for me to join her on the couch. She clicked on a table lamp, "I'd forgotten that I saved one of her letters. I think you should read it," she said.

I was stretched to the limit, as if the opposites were pulling me apart. Yet I made it to the couch in one piece and read:

*Mi Amiga,*
*I hope you are well. For me, it is a special day. July 22, the day my Andrés was born.*

My hand shook. The paper was crepey, the script small and tight, like mine. I glanced at Penny, who had started to knit, having gotten some needles and yarn from a nearby basket.

*I remember it well. I couldn't sleep, twisting and turning. It was so hot. The windows were wide open, but still so hot. My belly. Ay, ready to explode. Misery. I gave my husband much grief. It was so hot. The baby was supposed to be born two weeks earlier and I was so tired. So tired of waiting. My skin had wrinkles I never had before. I rubbed cocoa butter all over the belly, but it didn't help. I was angry, yelled at Carlos. He tried to comfort me, but I pushed him away. Then the pains finally came. I cried then too, for my mother, my father. Both dead. I was scared. I was so young. But Carlos, he was patient. He took me to the hospital and stayed as long as he could. Then he told me he would be in the waiting room.*
*The pain was so great. You know. But then, then my Andrés was born. Eight pounds! A full head of hair. He was the most*

*handsome baby. Muy guapo. The nurses said he would grow up to be a movie star. When they brought him to me, I cried. This time for joy. I swore I would be by his side forever. And I was. Until I was bad. Until I ruined his life.*

I read the words, but all I could feel was that stretch. From pity to fury, hate to love. But I kept reading.

*Did I tell you about the time Andrés almost drowned? We drove up to Lake Arrowhead. We brought a picnic lunch. We found a spot near the water. I unloaded the food, Carlos went to get a blanket and some toys from the car. Andrés was right next to me, already playing in the sand. He loved plants and trees. Loved to pick flowers and bring them to me. Ay, he was happy outdoors. Dios. He was right there beside me. But then suddenly, he was gone! In the lake! Before I knew it, in over his head. I didn't think, just ran in with my clothes on and got him. Ay. It was only a second, but he had already swallowed water and for a little bit didn't breathe. Never had I been so afraid. When he finally coughed, finally cried for me, I got on my knees and prayed. And I swore to live up to my name. Isabella. Devoted to God.*

I vaguely recalled being wrenched to the surface. Gasping for air.

*I've talked to you about it before, querida. But, please, let me tell you again.*

*Carlos was older than me. He thought about things. Cared about things. I cared mostly about myself. And Andrés. But I was only a girl, eighteen. And too pretty for my own good. I craved attention. Carlos was busy, always busy. And I was restless. I used to walk Andrés into the square, in the center of Boyle Heights. It was a busy place, with shops and movies and restaurants. Delicious smells. Lots of gossip. But I went for the whistles. Whistles and catcalls. And I got them. From men young and old and every type. Well, you know, especially one in particular. That Troy. He worked at the theater. Wore that spicy cologne. Blond, blue eyes. He used to wait for me to come. A gringo. I didn't care. In my house growing up, we didn't speak much Spanish. I had a lot of white friends. And this man. Troy...I can't even remember his last name. He was young, fun-loving. He danced, had a beautiful voice.*

*That day. Dios mío. I brought Andrés with me. Andrés was such a loving child. So sensitive. I hated to leave him with anyone. But Troy's sister, well, she was there that day, offered to take him for an ice cream. Just down the street. She babysat a lot. That day. September. Ninety degrees, I remember reading on a thermometer. It felt good in the cool theater. There we were in the balcony. In between shows. We were hugging and kissing. I didn't know what world I was in. And then, I looked up. I can see Carlos now. Standing there, slapping a rolled up newspaper on his leg. His eyes got very small. His lips disappeared. I thought he was going to beat me. Like a dog. But he just stood there as I covered myself up. Troy ran out. And still, Carlos didn't move. Finally, he said: "Where's Andrés?" That's all he said.*

*Penny. You've told me that we all make mistakes. That we are human. To stop feeling guilty. But I do, still. Still I think of my shame. That I deserved my punishment.*

Sterilized. She was saying she deserved to be sterilized. I turned the letter over.

*I know what you will say. But thank you. You always say it is good to talk, to write things down. And I do feel better. God bless my boy. I always remember his birthday. He is an important man, now. How I wish I'd been different. But you know, my dear, telling you. It helps.*

*Your friend, Isabella.*

Penny put her knitting down. "I know it's hard," she said.

I nodded.

"Andrew, you can now see," she said. "I couldn't leave her in that place. So she had a home here. And during that time, it still was you. Always about you that she talked. The sweet baby, the sensitive boy. The child who loved bedtime stories."

I remembered. Waiting in my bed, tucked under the covers. Waiting for my mother to read to me. Yes, I remembered.

"She wept over the pain she felt she'd inflicted. The wounds you must have suffered. I felt her pain, Andrew. And yours. When I came to L.A. I already felt I knew you. I already..."

Penny caught herself, looked away. Then she said: "Your mother became ill several months ago. I tried to tell you, then, the whole story."

"But I cut you off." I saw the knife again. Another kind of war. Cut. Dismembering a womb. Cut. Destroying my first home.

Snap.

~

*"Mijo, what is the creature that walks on four legs at dawn, two legs at noon, and three legs in the evening?"*

*"I don't know, Pop."*

*"Think, Mijo. Think."*

The first thing you should know is that I didn't faint. The wheelchair wasn't necessary. The second is that I wouldn't have known if I had because in the hours after Penny told me about my mother, I willed myself a full blown case of Cotard's. The kind that might be written up in that journal the doctor quoted. Dissolved. He simply dissolved, like an Alka Seltzer. Only my brain was left, alone, abandoned on a distant planet. The other thing, though, is that I wasn't frightened. I wasn't in pain. I hadn't been devoured. I'd just disappeared, and I knew it.

What I also knew, however, was that I'd be in agony when I decided to return. Because this time each atom would have to maintain its shape. Each fact would have to be nailed down. There would be no more back and forth. And I would only be ready for that when I was strong enough to hold a hammer.

It took two weeks. During that time, Penny came and went. I saw her, heard her, smelled her. I felt her feed me, wipe me down with a cool cloth. I was conscious of everything, yet far, far away.

~

*"Man. It's Man, Pop! Crawling on all fours as a baby, standing on two feet as an adult and using a cane in old age."*

*"Right, Mijo. That's right!"*

~

It was a Sunday when I remembered how I'd answered that riddle, the one my father had taught me. And the irony wasn't lost on me. The day of rest would be my hardest yet.

I wanted to stay gone, stay lost on that planet. But my blood was flowing, coursing through my veins. I no longer had a choice. I was back in my body, with all that implied.

The clock read eleven. I sat up and checked my limbs. A few bruises. Weak, but strong enough, I supposed, to hold a hammer. I called for Penny, who had the nails.

~

Penny sat down on the bed. The mattress squeaked. "You look better," she said, the Sphinx-like expression replaced with the look of a wide open door.

"I'm here, anyway."

~

Penny said that my mother harbored no animosity toward my father. Why should she? He loved her and she'd betrayed him. She blamed herself. But she ached for her son, prayed for him nightly. She'd kept tabs on me, Penny said, through the papers. And secretly through one of the picker's wives. Through this woman she learned much about me. That I had an odd medical condition, that my best friend had been killed, that I had become a lawyer.

Kept tabs? That shocked me perhaps more than anything.

"As I told you, Andrew, I met her after her procedure. She was despondent, had lost the will to live. But when she spoke of you, her face lit up. "Here," Penny said, handing me a yellowed photograph. "She kept this with her always, was clutching it when she died."

I took the photo, still wincing. Bleeding where the nails dug in. Except that it was my mother, not me, who'd been the sacrifice. I looked at the photo. She was holding me, leaning against the tree outside our home. Dark and lovely, nuzzling my neck. She wore a sleeveless dress, willowy arms exposed, waving with one hand, to my father no doubt.

I looked closer. My aunt in Oaxaca. Yes, same coloring, same eyes. Now I understood. That was the familiarity, the resemblance. She must have been my mother's sister. Not my father's. She was kind to me, but no doubt felt disgraced by my mother, too, enough to go along with my father's deception.

"When your mother got sick," Penny said, "I was desperate. She'd forbidden me to contact you, never wanted you to know about her. But I needed to do something. For her. For you. For myself."

"I'm glad you did," I said, although even now it was hard to admit.

"There's one more thing I'd like to show you," Penny said, scooting away the wheelchair. She offered me her arm, which, though wrapped in the softest of wool, felt like an anchor. We walked upstairs and outside, past the nursery, where the muffled cries that would have normally not registered now made me well up.

"This is where your mother stayed," Penny said, as we arrived at a small bungalow. "She liked being near the babies. There used to be a couch, a table and a bed in here. It was plain, but your mother was happy for it."

The room was now empty, save for a folding chair and wooden chest.

"Her belongings are in there," she said. "Take your time."

I sat down on the chair and for several minutes stared at the blank walls, imagining my mother. Waking and sleeping, thinking and dreaming. Frail, full of regret. And then I remembered the store window again. Only now I knew what it meant. The reason for my father's anger. The source of the gloom that he transferred to me that Halloween. It wasn't an illness. No terminal malady. It was a lie, not a disease.

I ran my hand over the trunk and undid the latch, half expecting my mother's spirit to materialize like a pent-up genie.

~

What to make of these things? Objects for the Goodwill, the Salvation Army. Hand-me-downs. Meaningless, tattered everyday objects.

There was a pair of shoes. Black, orthopedic, with scraggly laces. I held one up, looked inside. The darkened pressure points of a foot. How many miles had it walked? On how many surfaces? I could just make out the size. Five. Mine were an eleven.

Next a hat, blue felt with a yellow feather. Once stylish, now faded. The feather made me think of Emerson. And Gringo. The refuge. My mother said I loved to be outdoors. And I did. What happened to me? I hadn't gone to a lake or the mountains or even the nearby ocean in years. Just that little glimpse out the office window.

The hat was small and dainty. A strand of white hair clung to it. Another, and another.

Dresses. Two of them. Both drab. High necked. Not the kind she wore into the Boyle Heights square. These wouldn't elicit a whistle. I bristled, felt a wisp of anger. But she was just a girl.

A flowered jacket with shoulder pads. It must have hung on her tiny frame.

Her purse. Rather large, greyer than it must have originally been. A dull silver buckle and zipper. I opened it. Empty, but it smelled minty. Huh. That smell. My mother used to suck on candies, didn't she? Her version of a stick. I think I once swallowed one whole.

A watch. Cheap. Cracked glass. Marking the passage of time. So much time. I shook it, twisted the knob. Didn't work. Did it ever? And a rosary. Blue with missing beads. Did she hold this, too, as she died?

I examined the items again. Rolled them in my hands, sniffed the mothballed past.

A few more. A ratty, terrycloth robe. Trousers that looked like they'd never been worn. A smaller pair of trousers. Much smaller. Faded red corduroy with a hole in the knee...

Those trousers were mine! The ones I wore that Halloween I'd dressed up as a fireman. My father was holding my hand, wearing his grim reaper expression. My mother walked silently behind us, her costume an invisible shroud. I remember pretending to put out a blaze, running from one burning house to another. And then I tripped. Fell hard on my knee, ripping my pants.

I limped home that night, and was still limping the next week when my father told me my mother had died. Unexpectedly. Suddenly. Sick. Nobody's fault.

Could I see her? No. Attend the funeral? No. Too young, my father said. Naturally I was upset, but didn't understand, didn't experience the full weight of the loss until I could no longer smell her. Until repeated cleanings removed any trace of her scent.

All those years. Somehow keeping this tattered memento. Red, like the blood that united us. Her *niño*'s trousers. I imagined her hugging them, crying into them like a handkerchief. Like I was doing now. Wiping her nose on the waist, drying her cheek on the hem. Remembering me wearing them.

I took off my shoes, stuck my feet into the little boy legs. Then I reached for my mother's hat, tilted it on my head. Pulled her sweater through my arms, dangled her rosary around my neck. I laughed through my tears, dressed up in holiday attire. This wasn't Halloween, with its monsters and horror shows, with fright as its primary objective. I was remembering and celebrating, honoring the past that had haunted me. It was my own personal Day of the Dead.

"Oh! I'm so sorry." Penny stood in the doorway, turning to leave.

"No," I said. "Please. Don't go."

# 24

## V-E DAY

"Andrew Martin, Esquire, Andrew Martin Esquire!"

I glanced at Emerson in my rearview mirror. He'd clearly had enough of this drive, resorting to repetitions that he knew had started to annoy me. I'd tried to teach him my real name, the one that would grace the shingle of my new office, but he would have none of it. The move to Stockton would be all he could stand. He knew me for what I was and was too set in his ways to change.

"We'll be there very soon," I said, reaching back and handing him a piece of pear through his cage.

It wasn't until I got back to L.A. that I'd learned that David, the paperboy, had found my bird. He hadn't known that Emerson was missing, hadn't seen the ad in the Lost and Found, never saw Martha or knew anything about her. I'd stopped my delivery before leaving, of course, but I was on his route so he regularly biked by. One day, he thought he spotted Emerson's green head in a nearby Jacaranda, but wrote it off to a blowing leaf. It simply couldn't be. But he couldn't quite put the thought to rest either, so every day thereafter, he brought some treat with him and called out his name.

Emerson showed himself cautiously. David tried to find me, reported a lost parrot, but heard nothing. By that time, Martha had given up. So he took Emerson home and waited. He left a note on my porch that, despite the recent Santa Ana winds, had somehow stayed put.

Our reunion was fraught. At first, Emerson seemed to not believe his eyes or his beak. He tentatively gnawed on my nose. When he was convinced it was me, he was more annoyed than happy. Moreover, he had become attached to David. I thought I might have to surrender him to the boy. But gradually he came around. And David was relieved. "Your bird," he said, "is a pain."

The trip to Stockton had been relatively quick, especially considering Emerson's antics and the small trailer hitched to the back. I'd glided over the Tejon Pass partly because the weather was clear but also because my car was new. A 1950 Oldsmobile with Hydramatic transmission. No shifting gears, and I hadn't had to stop for gas until I was long past the café and the field and the brothel, until the twisted road of last winter gave way to a straighter path ahead.

It was fall. October 12th, my anniversary once again. My apartment was vacant, awaiting the young renter who would no doubt paint the walls a brighter color.

L.A. seemed to yawn as I left, tired of my presence, indifferent to my departure. I waved, but no one was there to see me off. Not John, who was on a vacation with Cici, and certainly not Frank.

I'd heard from Hiram. He told me that a few days after I'd given him the pamphlet, the couple, whose real names they still didn't know, abandoned the house. They'd managed to escape without notice, he said, probably during the one night when surveillance was spotty. As of yet, there'd been so sign of them. But based on my discoveries, Hiram had convinced a noteworthy reporter, a man named Langford (who, according to Hiram, was, in appearance, the epitome of the Aryan ideal), to conduct an investigation.

Langford began at *Turn Verein*, the German Club, gaining entrance by saying his paper wanted to do a story on the upcoming *Harmonie* show. The Club's president was delighted, Langford said, and introduced him to the relevant members. Langford told Hiram that the place was convivial, providing camaraderie for people of German descent. His first impression was that there was nothing suspicious. Indeed, he was even more convinced of that after casually mentioning Joe and Claire. No one had heard of them, and they seemed to be telling the truth.

But on his way out, something happened that upped the ante.

He had parked on J Street, a block down from the building. As he approached his car, three men appeared to be waiting for him. They were all tall, bulky and wearing suits.

"Can I help you?" Langford asked.

"Yes. Better lay off," one of them answered.

"Who are you?" Langford said, "and what are you talking about?"

The same man then got in Langford's face and said, "What you're doing could be very unhealthy for you. And your family."

"What do you mean?"

"Let's just say we know where your kid goes to school. You go write about something else, you hear?"

And with that, they left.

Whether they were members of the Club, the Secret Service or the FBI didn't matter. Langford was now certain there was merit to Hiram's claim. There would indeed be a column to write, and it wouldn't involve *Harmonie*. After that, he hired protection and continued to investigate. He learned that both Joe and Claire had an extraordinary aptitude for languages, that they were not born in the Midwest and that they had made a number of phone calls to Germany. He hadn't yet confirmed the exact role the couple played, or whether Joe was, in fact, another Mengele. But he vowed the story, whatever it was, would go to print.

~

Am I cured? Has the truth set me free? Not entirely. My leg still gives me trouble. It's a habit, I guess, a crutch for which I may always need a cane. And I was still on high alert as the anniversary approached. I'd stocked up on rum, renewed my Miltown prescription, and slept with one eye on the calendar. But the day broke gently. The shadows were lighter, the volume turned down. And I didn't even visit the cemetery, only drove by before turning onto 99.

In the trailer were my Danish chair, covered with my grandmother's blanket, and few other odds and ends I didn't trust to the movers. Emerson's cage was in the back seat, squished between my clothes. I hoped they would have served as a buffer, but maybe nothing would have comforted him. He coughed and spit out the pear on the shoulder of my best jacket.

I pushed down on the pedal, amazed at the smooth touch. It was dusk, the sky a dappled pink. Dappled. That's what I was, what the past months had done to me. Spotting me with color, altering my background, my point of view. My father's image still loomed large, but it was now in a malleable frame. Learning about my mother had jarred something loose. I was the tin man after being oiled, after visiting Oz. My limbs still creaked, but I could stretch. My instinct was still to judge, to take the winner's side. But I'd been given a heart. Fragile, but beating. And a heart was what women like my mother, like the girls at the Home, needed.

Heart and skills, which is why I'd decided mine would be

better served helping them, the women who one way or another had helped me. Beginning with Penny. I thought I'd blown out the spark, smothered it with my fear and denial. But I didn't know then about survival. About the real meaning of salvation.

Stockton. Twenty miles. I felt a surge of adrenalin. Up and down my spine, through my gut, out my fingers. Like a schoolboy. Twenty miles. I'd had to travel much farther than that to get to where I was.

It was difficult for Penny and me to acknowledge our feelings for one another, even though they'd been dancing on the surface, thinning the ice, waiting for the first crack. After the letters, the photos, the trunk, after everything she'd done for me, it still almost didn't happen.

When I asked Penny to stay with me that day in my mother's room, I'd meant it. I yearned for her company. But when she obliged, sat down beside me with everything strewn about, with bits of myself strewn about, I choked. The screen re-ascended. She'd seen me at my worst, peeled down to the core. Yes, I admired her. Desired her. But maybe it was only gratitude. Confusing one kind of emotion with another.

"Well," she said.

"Well."

"What now?"

"I'll go," I said. "Time to get back to my life." It's not what I wanted, but saying it made me feel stronger, in charge.

Penny's mouth dropped, which I supposed is exactly what I'd hoped. But she quickly regained her composure. "Yes," she replied, "I think that's best."

Neither of us was experienced in love so we almost lost the chance for it. I packed that night and quickly said my good-byes the next morning. I sped away. But I only got as far as the 101 turn-off. Penny. Her face kept flashing before me. I blinked but the image wouldn't leave. Something she said had stuck in my mind. Or rather something she hadn't said. I stopped for coffee and sat in the car for an hour. It would mean looking needy, inconsistent. Weak again. But panic seized me, along with a realization. This was my one shot. Those stars had finally aligned, but they wouldn't do so twice.

I drove back to Fairhaven and parked. Doubts crept in, but this was no time to think. The moment called for action.

"Mr. Martin! Rachel said.

"I need to see Penny."

"One of the girls is in labor. Penny's at the hospital."

A replay. Christ. "Can I wait?"

Rachel led me again to the sewing room. Another replay. Only this time I wasn't in a wheel chair. I headed to the familiar window and stood looking out. A lazy sun had taken the moon's place. I turned to the girls, who regarded me mildly, as if I were a fixture in the room. All except for Lucy, who smiled at me like the Cheshire Cat.

"Hello there," she said, walking toward me, her belly protruding farther than only a few days ago. "Still here?"

Damn if she wasn't impertinent.

"Yeah. Still working."

"We've heard differently."

"Oh?"

"Uh huh. But, well, none of my business."

"What is your business?"

"My business? Like I told you before, I want to improve places like this."

So she was still on that kick.

"Help girls in trouble," she said. "Organize. You know, if girls need an alternative," she whispered, "I think they should have it. Shouldn't be illegal, if you know what I mean."

*I tried to do away with it. Didn't work out.*

"What do you think, Mr. Martin?"

I looked into her young eyes. Young, but brimming with nerve, and wisdom perhaps. Organize. The first time I'd heard that word and not bled. "To tell the truth, Lucy, I haven't given it much thought."

But I'd started to. Started to think, then and there, about what was just, what was right. For these girls and others. For women like Cici, Penny, my mother. What was just. And who should decide. Thorny questions, and I didn't have the answers. But I resolved to get them.

When Penny entered the sewing room, she looked right through me. Rachel had obviously told her I was there, but something else was on her mind. Something more important, more doleful than my abrupt return. She was pale and drawn. "Sandra didn't make it," she said.

Gasps. Dropped needles. The girls gathered around her.

"She hemorrhaged."

The girls cried and hugged. They were heartbroken and afraid.

"How's the baby?" Lucy said.

"Fine. A healthy girl."

I was still standing by the window, watching. Out of place. An intruder, interloper. A man.

After a bit, Penny walked over to me. "What are you doing here?"

"I'm so sorry," I said.

"Yes. Very sad. Damn law. She should have been allowed to terminate the pregnancy. These girls need options, not punishment. Not shame."

I was beginning to agree.

"Well?" she said.

"Can we talk somewhere else?"

"Later."

When later came, I about lost my nerve. Penny looked exhausted. How could I talk about us after what she'd been through? But how could I not?

I exhaled and took her hands in mine: "Penny, yesterday you started to say something. You said you felt you already knew me, that you already... And then you stopped. What did you already?"

"No," she said. "You're going to have to go first."

I didn't know if I could do it. Words really can stick in your throat. I swallowed, once, twice. "I need you in my life."

She slowly smiled. "You've come a long way, Mr. Martin. All right. I said I felt I knew you. Knew you the way your mother did. And what I almost said? That I loved you, in that way, too."

"And now?"

She looked away. "I don't know."

But over the next few months, filled with fits and starts, awkward moments, and intimacy neither of us thought possible, she did know. We both knew. Love, the kind you wanted to last, arrived. Despite our differences, our pain, our secrets, we had found in each other what we'd never had alone: a feeling of belonging.

After that, the way forward was clear. We would marry. I would move. Establish the new business. What would it be? I still wasn't sure. I just wanted the next Sandra to live.

We even found a house, one that with some expanding could serve as an office. I still had that hitchhiker's card. The architect. Maybe I'd give him a call.

We'd agreed on something else, too. Something powerful.

Something so big that I feared it might lay me low again. But it was just the opposite. It lifted me, quite literally, on a flight to New York. And it was funny. Cici wasn't glad to see me. Until I told her why I'd come.

~

I envisioned Penny waiting for me now, her wheat hair freed from the bonnet, lending sustenance as well as beauty to the landscape. Waiting at our house, near the Home. I could see her. Adoption papers filed away. Holding my daughter. Our daughter, Isabella.

And it was no dream.

"Andrew Martin, Esquire! Andrew Martin, Esquire!"

"Andrés Martínez, you crazy bird."

# AUTHOR'S NOTE

There is a heated debate in literary circles today regarding who should be able to speak for whom. Specifically, are authors justified in portraying characters of backgrounds—race, class, gender, etc.—different from their own? The question is valid, given literature's history as the exclusive domain of white men. The playing field has been long in need of some leveling. As a Jewish woman with grandchildren of mixed race, I understand the concerns. I grappled with it in writing this book, as my protagonist is Latino.

My own answer centers on intent. What is the author trying to achieve in writing from the perspective of the Other? In my case, I was trying to inhabit a character from my previous book, then a young man, now an adult. I was trying to understand him, to walk in his shoes. As indeed I was for the rest of the characters, none of whom share my identical experience. It will be for readers to decide whether the portrayals ring true.

# ACKNOWLEDGEMENTS

In the book's early stages, I'd been looking for a unique way to physically represent my protagonist's internal conflict. By chance, I heard an interview on NPR that ended my search. Scientist Anil Anathaswanmy was discussing his new book, *The Man Who Wasn't There*. I listened rapt and ordered it immediately. It was in this marvelous work that I learned about Cotard's syndrome. I am also indebted to Eric Lichtblau's Pulitzer Prize winning history: *The Nazis Next Door*. Many other texts informed the story, too numerous to mention.

The list of writers, friends, and family to whom I owe thanks can't be sufficently addressed here. Each contributed to the completion of the book in his or her own way, and I am deeply grateful. They are: Sally Pla, Janice Steinberg, Abbie Padgett, Linda Felder, Carolyn Marsden, Sarah Sleeper, Dare Delano, Teri Abbott Watson, John Penfield, Nancy Miller, Amy Wallen, Tracy Richmond, Chet Koblinsky, Don Davis, Jim Wales, Lauren Kahn, Jeff Kahn, Charles Holland, Robert Laurence, Brooke Fruchtman, and Dan Howard.

A special thanks to Benjamin Russell for his superb editing and to former *Los Angeles Times* book critic and author David Ulin for the mini MFA. And, of course, to James Clois Smith, Jr. of Sunstone Press for once again believing in and publishing my work.

To my husband, Dean, I can't say enough. Technical skill, multiple readings and edits that I begrudgingly accepted as better than my own. More than anything, for his love and the patience that I sorely lack.

And a final thanks to Rhoda Kantor and Douglas Rosenbaum. And they know why.

## READER'S GUIDE

1. Discuss the relevance of the three quotes that begin the novel.

2. The novel echoes Homer's *Odyssey*. How? Identify specific allusions to the epic and discuss their relevance to the story.

3. Discuss the nature of Andrew's condition. How does it reflect his identity conflict?

4. Discuss the female characters and the general role of women in the novel.

5. Does the author's portrayal of the 1940s conform to your image of this historical period? If so, in what ways? If not, why?

6. Talk about Emerson. Why is he so important to Andrew?

7. What does Andrew learn about himself in the A.W.O.L. chapter?

8. By the end of the novel, Andrew has evolved. How? In what ways is he the same?

9. Is Andrew a sympathetic character? Why or why not?

10. Discuss the Nazi episode with respect to Andrew's quest.

11. Using the portrayal of Fairhaven as a point of comparison, discuss the challenges women faced then as opposed to now.

12. What are some of the novel's themes? How does the author treat them?

CPSIA information can be obtained
at www.ICGtesting.com
Printed in the USA
FSHW010007220721
83348FS

9 781632 932983